# "I Just Wanted To Repay You For Rescuing Me This Morning,"

Cass said, trying to retain her composure in the face of this sexy, rugged man.

He raised one eyebrow at her, studying her with intensity.

"Well, now that you mention it, there is one thing I'd like."

His eyes narrowed and his gaze swept slowly down her body, sending signals to parts that had lain dormant for a long time. Cass fidgeted and stepped away from Rafe's warmth.

"What *do* you want?"

"You," he said.

\* \* \* \* \* \* \* \* \*

"A wonderful new voice is added to the Desire line. Katherine Garbera blends humor, warmth and sizzling sexual tension in *The Bachelor Next Door*. I'm looking forward to her next book…and the next…."

—Bestselling author Pamela Macaluso

Dear Reader,

### LET'S CELEBRATE FIFTEEN YEARS
### OF SILHOUETTE DESIRE...

with some of your favorite authors and new stars of tomorrow.
For the next three months, we present a spectacular lineup
of unforgettably romantic love stories—led by three
MAN OF THE MONTH titles.

In October, Diana Palmer returns to Desire with
*The Patient Nurse,* which features an unforgettable hero.
Next month, Ann Major continues her bestselling CHILDREN
OF DESTINY series with *Nobody's Child.* And in December,
Dixie Browning brings us her special brand of romantic
charm in *Look What the Stork Brought.*

But Desire is not only MAN OF THE MONTH! It's new
love stories from talented authors Christine Rimmer,
Helen R. Myers, Raye Morgan, Metsy Hingle and new star
Katherine Garbera in October.

In November, don't miss sensuous surprises from BJ James,
Lass Small, Susan Crosby, Eileen Wilks and Shawna Delacorte.

And December will be filled with Christmas cheer from
Maureen Child, Kathryn Jensen, Christine Pacheco,
Anne Eames and Barbara McMahon.

Remember, here at Desire we've been committed to bringing
you the very best in unforgettable romance and sizzling
sensuality. And to add to the excitement of fifteen wonderful
years, we offer the chance for you to win some wonderful
prizes. Look in the pages at the end of the book for details.

And may we have many more years of happy reading together!

*Melissa Senate*

Senior Editor

---

Please address questions and book requests to:
Silhouette Reader Service
U.S.: 3010 Walden Ave., P.O. Box 1325, Buffalo, NY 14269
Canadian: P.O. Box 609, Fort Erie, Ont. L2A 5X3

# KATHERINE GARBERA
## THE BACHELOR NEXT DOOR

SILHOUETTE *Desire*

Published by Silhouette Books

America's Publisher of Contemporary Romance

For Matt, best friend, lover and husband—without your support and belief in me, I couldn't have done it. And for my children, Courtney and Lucas, who make me remember why we're here.

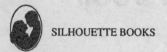 SILHOUETTE BOOKS

ISBN 0-373-76104-X

THE BACHELOR NEXT DOOR

Copyright © 1997 by Katherine Garbera

Printed in U.S.A.

## *KATHERINE GARBERA*

has always enjoyed creating stories. She is a member of Romance Writers of America and has served on her local chapter's board as president and treasurer. She's had a varied career path, including: lifeguard, production page, VIP tour guide and secretary. Reading, shopping, playing the flute and counted cross-stitch are just some of her hobbies. She's always believed that everything she dreams she can do. With the support of her husband, daughter and family, she wrote her first novel and found she had to write another one. In 1995 she won the Georgia Romance Writers Maggie Award for excellence in unpublished short contemporary writing. In a world that is so technologically advanced, Katherine believes we need more romance in our daily lives and hopes to create that with her novels.

# The Silhouette Spotlight
## "Where Passion Lives"

MEET WOMAN TO WATCH *Katherine Garbera*

### What was your inspiration for THE BACHELOR NEXT DOOR?

KG: "My family. In developing my hero and heroine, that importance of family came across. I especially needed a key to who Rafe Santini was. Rafe had a strong sense of family...so I took his family away from him and left him with the guilt of their deaths. The want of a family is still strong within Rafe, but he believes he will destroy anyone he cares for."

### What about the Desire line appeals to you as a reader and as a writer?

KG: "It's fast paced, sometimes serious and sometimes funny, but always sensual."

### Why is this book special to you?

KG: "Because of Rafe Santini. I fell in love with the lonely playboy who lives across the street from the heroine and her son. While I was writing this book, for the first time I was able to deal honestly with the emotions my characters were feeling. I learned a lot about myself as a writer from it. I set the story in Florida where I was born and raised, because I love this state."

### Any additional information about yourself or your book?

KG: "After I won the Georgia Romance Writers Maggie Award for this book, I was serenaded by an entire Marine Corps unit in the bar. It was very exciting and fun."

# One

"Mommy's trapped in the bathroom and I've got to get to school."

Rafe Santini ran a hand over his bleary eyes, willing the tiny apparition standing in his doorway to disappear. A quick glance at his battered watch confirmed that it was 7:00 a.m. He scratched the stubble on his chin and stretched his arms above his head before looking down again.

The boy was still there. Rafe knew nothing about children and liked it that way. This child had invaded his private retreat, and though Rafe knew he should regret the intrusion, part of him was intrigued by the situation.

"Come on, mister. Will you help me?" The boy's eyes were teary, and Rafe feared the child would start crying.

Rafe leaned against the front door frame and sighed. Ah, hell, he couldn't leave the child in the lurch. "Okay, okay. Give me a minute."

Rafe slid his feet into the buffalo sandals he'd left on the porch for late-night walks with his dog. He scratched his bare chest, debating whether he had time to grab a shirt before leaving, then decided the kid looked too desperate for even a minute's delay. The boy lived directly across the street from Rafe. He'd seen the kid on the front porch studying, when he went for his daily jog.

The yard was neat and tidy, no toys, bikes or plastic pools littered the grounds. In fact, there was no evidence that a kid lived there, much less a young boy.

A battered Volvo wagon stood in the driveway. The boy grabbed Rafe's hand, hurrying him along. The door opened smoothly and a fresh floral scent beckoned him closer.

The house was laid out similarly to his, except all of the remodeling had been completed. The hardwood floor shone brightly under handwoven rugs. The banister on the stairs had been cleaned until the details of the intricate carvings were clearly visible. His banister was still covered with years of dirt and grime, but he hoped it would be in the same condition as this one when he removed the layers of filth.

"Andy! Where are you?" called a worried voice from upstairs. "You better get back up here pronto."

*Pronto?* Who used that word anymore? Rafe smiled at the frazzled sound of the woman's voice. It reminded him of his mother's when he'd been into mischief. The grin on the boy's face mirrored Rafe's own.

"Andy." Anger was clear in the voice now. Amusement slid from the boy's face like a rain cloud covering the sun.

"We'd better hurry." The kid scrambled up the stairs, Rafe followed. They stopped outside the hall in front of the bathroom door.

"Don't worry, Mommy. I brought help."

"Who? The only person you're allowed to speak to is on vacation."

"It's okay. I got the man from across the street. The one you said had nice buns."

"Andy," the voice protested, taking on a squeaky quality.

Rafe ignored that comment, figuring he'd better help the lady out of the bathroom before she exploded out of there in a killer rage. He grinned, thinking there were worse ways to be woken up. Maybe this wasn't going to be such a bad day.

Rafe returned his attention to the door. The problem appeared to be a small, plastic army's front row of soldiers wedged under it. "Reenacting a battle?"

A row of perfect white teeth were revealed when the boy smiled. "Yeah, Gettysberg. We're studying the Civil War in school."

"Andy the word is *yes*, not *yeah*. Please save the war stories for another time." Again the voice from behind the door. "The problem isn't on the battlefield, the lock is stuck."

"Sorry, Mommy."

"That's okay, Andy. I think a bobby pin ought to work."

"I'm fresh out of bobby pins," Rafe said.

She'd calmed down now, and her voice had lost the frazzled, worried quality. The woman's voice was straight out of his dreams. Distant dreams that he hadn't allowed himself to think of in years. A sweet voice that reminded him of church on Sunday mornings and lazy days spent in bed. Images of home and family danced through his mind before he firmly shut them out.

"But I'll improvise. Do you have a screwdriver?" he asked.

"Downstairs in the kitchen. What are you planning to do?"

The worried edge had returned to her voice, and he also detected a hint of resentment. Rafe wondered how long she'd been trapped in the bathroom. She was probably apprehensive about having a stranger in her house and the boy being alone with him. But he wasn't a rapist or ax murderer and he *was* trying to rescue her. She'd just have to take what she got from him.

"Go get it for me, Andy." The boy moved quickly to do Rafe's bidding.

He bent to examine the doorknob and the lock. Rafe had always had a knack for fixing things and had spent his adult life working in construction. The old-fashioned handle would make taking it apart easier than a newer model would have been. But he wasn't as sure of the inner workings.

"Excuse me, sir. Are you still out there?" Her voice was prim and proper now, almost cold with formality. Where had the soft, sweet tone disappeared to?

"Yes, ma'am." He drawled out the words in a way he'd been told was annoying. Two could play at this game. In fact, he wagered he would win the manners match.

"What are you planning to do?" she asked, sounding slightly less uptight.

"I'm going to remove the doorknob. If that doesn't work I'll have to take the door off its hinges." He wondered what she looked like.

"I'd rather you didn't remove the door."

That cold tone was beginning to grate on his already strained nerves. "Hell, I'd rather not remove the door, either. But unless you want to spend the day in there, I might have to."

"I'll thank you not to curse. Andy's at an age where he's easily influenced."

He grunted instead of replying, not knowing what type of response that comment warranted. All he wanted to do now was get her out of the bathroom and leave. He grinned. She probably felt anxious about his knowing her opinion of his buns. "Sit tight, lady."

Remarkably, she was silent for a few minutes. He could hear her pacing in the small bathroom. Once she saw him face-to-face she would put more distance between them than the ocean between continents. He wasn't the type of man women wanted their young sons around. Which was okay by him. He didn't particularly want to be around kids, anyway.

"Who are you?" she asked. Her voice calmer now, almost resigned.

"Don't you know?"

Silence stretched. "We've never met."

"Rafe Santini. I'm your new neighbor across the street." He pulled his Swiss Army knife from his pocket and scratched at the empty keyhole. He wanted a clear view of the inner locking mechanism. "How long have you been locked in?"

"About an hour. I was taking a bath. I like to soak for a while." She paused, clearing her throat. "Mr. Santini, um…I didn't mean to sound ungrateful—"

"Here you go," Andy said, returning with the screwdriver.

Rafe removed the doorknob. It should have taken only five minutes, but Andy wanted to know everything that was happening and asked questions incessantly.

Rafe remembered doing the same thing to his father as a child. Those memories gave him the patience to answer all of the boy's questions. Andy was smart and never asked the same thing twice, which amazed Rafe.

Once the knob was removed, it was easy to open the door. Rafe had expected the woman to be matronly, round and soft like his mom had been. The woman had a son and a formal tone of voice that reminded him of his spinster aunt Florence. But instead, Andy's mother was—ah, hell, his mind fought against the word *attractive*. Dammit, she was sexy.

Her dark brown hair was piled on top of her head. Tendrils curled around her heart-shaped face, the sable locks contrasting with the light, creamy color of her skin. Her eyes were a gingery color that made him think of fall leaves, Thanksgiving and home. The thin, pink silk robe she wore did little to disguise her feminine curves. She was one hell of a temptation, and he cursed himself for noticing.

She stepped on one of Andy's frontline soldiers and hopped on one foot before losing her balance. Rafe snapped out of his trance and caught her in his arms.

She was a light, tempting bundle, and for a moment he forgot everything else—the child, the anger, her ridiculous opinion of his buns. Everything but the fact that she was a woman. And it had been too long since he'd held a woman in his arms. A woman who had more than a fleeting thought drifting through her head. A woman who smelled sweet, not like cheap perfume and cheaper whiskey. A woman who was trying her damnedest to get out of his arms.

"Please, put me down." The formal tone again.

"Sure."

He set her on her feet well away from the Rebel Army, and she gathered her dignity around her like a heavy winter cloak. Ridiculous, considering that she wore nothing but a thin piece of silk, which was clinging to her body like a second skin.

"Thank you," she said, turning to Rafe. "I'm Cassandra Gambrel. You've met Andy."

Her voice sounded soft and sweet again, which surprised him. He'd expected her to stick with the formal tone. The hand she held out was fine boned, making him feel large and masculine. The nails were painted in a delicate shell pink color that perfectly matched the natural color of her lips. He was in big trouble.

"Rafe Santini," he said, finishing the introductions she'd begun.

"Thank you for rescuing me," she said, clutching the lapels of her robe together.

This woman's skin was the creamiest he'd ever seen. Would it taste as good? He wanted to put his mouth to the pulse beating strongly in her neck and taste it. "I'll put the knob back for you."

"The lock sticks," Cassandra said. "Usually if I wait long enough it loosens."

"I'll fix it," he said, needing the distraction.

"You should get dressed, Mommy."

Cassandra nodded, then walked down the hall, stopping at the end. "Don't get in the way, Andy."

"Aw, Mom."

Rafe chuckled to himself, remembering how it had been to be growing up and fighting against the ties to your parents.

Andy nodded sagely. "I'm the man of the house now, but Mommy doesn't let me do that much stuff."

"Moms are like that."

Andy sighed, sounding years older than he was. "Yeah, they are."

Rafe's attention drifted from the open door and Andy to the woman walking down the hall. Her stride was soft and smooth and her hips swayed temptingly…ah, hell.

Once in her own bedroom, Cass dressed hurriedly, throwing on the first thing she encountered. She rushed through her routine in front of the mirror, not wanting to slow down for fear she'd start thinking about *him.*

Rafe Santini's backside was a sight to behold, but he was even more heart stopping from the front. His eyes were a brilliant gray that made her think of glaciers—but with fire burning inside them. His hair was thick, curly, and her fingers tingled with the desire to touch it. His bare chest caused her blood to beat ninety to nothing. She swiftly braided her hair and stuffed her feet into a pair of scuffed Top-Siders.

*The one you said had nice buns.* The words echoed in her mind like an executioner's voice asking for last requests. She wanted to die of embarrassment, but that was the least of her problems.

She didn't like the way Andy had been staring up at Mr. Santini. Like he was some sort of hero, or worse yet, a candidate for a father. Andy had a way of sizing up men that made them scurry to leave, or look at her in a different light. And if Mr. Santini thought of her as a woman, she had a sinking feeling that the prospects for her survival wouldn't be good.

Since her husband's death two years ago, Andy had been looking for a replacement daddy. It was nothing overt, but more the quiet contemplation of each and every single man they met. She knew Andy well enough to know that he would probe into Mr. Santini's background while they worked. Andy would dig into the man's past with all the enthusiasm of a paleontologist about to uncover a rare dinosaur bone.

Cass hated that she had to apologize to Rafe Santini but knew she owed it to him. She'd been rude. He'd sounded annoyed when she'd questioned him, but she was used to being in charge, used to being the one responsible for solving all of their family problems. It was weird being rescued by a man.

She planned on ignoring the comment Andy had repeated, and if the man had any couth he'd do the same. Besides, what man wanted to talk about his backside?

She stepped into the hall and watched, amazed to see Mr. Santini's patience with her son. It was obvious to her that he'd had no contact with children on a daily basis. His language was deplorable, as if he didn't realize that young ears waited to test and try every new word they heard. Yet, he made the effort to be friendly with her son, and some of her discomfort melted away.

Andy's curiosity was insatiable. He drove his grandmother nearly insane with his questions. Sometimes he even managed to get on *her* nerves with his demands to know how everything worked. But this stranger, this man, was dealing patiently with Andy. Cass felt a softening near her heart.

She cleared her throat, and they both turned to look at her. "Can I offer you a cup of coffee, Mr. Santini?"

"Yes, ma'am."

Cassandra hated to be called ma'am but figured she

should hold her tongue after her earlier ungracious behavior. "Andy, go get ready for school."

"But, Mommy—"

"Now, please."

She watched her child walk toward his bedroom looking as if the weight of the world was on his shoulders. Then she turned to Santini. "Are you done here?"

"Just about. You need to get a new knob. I removed the lock, though, so you won't get trapped in there again."

His silver-gray eyes seemed brilliant in the dim light of the hallway. She'd never stood this close to a man as virile as Rafe Santini. His muscles were well defined, but not overdeveloped. She was suddenly aware of how long it had been since she'd exercised. He made her feel shabby and out of shape.

"I'm ready for that coffee now."

"Sure, follow me."

His footsteps sounded heavy on the stairs as he followed her down and into her kitchen. She'd used a sunflower border to brighten the room and had purchased all of her accessories with the same motif in mind. She thought her kitchen was sunny and welcoming, but seeing Rafe there made her question that thought. He looked out of place and uncomfortable.

Instead of sitting at the café-style table in the corner, he leaned one hip against the kitchen counter. He was dressed in faded jeans that clung to his muscled legs like a glove, accentuating their length and leanness. His bare chest was even more tempting than those gorgeous buns of his. She imagined Rafe as a big cat lying in wait for prey, and tried to convince herself she bore no resemblance to a mouse.

Lust at first sight, her mind said. God, the man was gorgeous. It wasn't fair that he should look like an ad for decadence and hard living after talking to her son with kindness and consideration.

Rafe made her nervous. It had been too many years since a man had lounged in her kitchen, waiting for the coffee to finish brewing. She wondered if he'd comment on the lightness of the brew the way Carl always had.

"Thanks for coming to the rescue," she said, needing to fill the silence. Small talk wasn't her forte, but she knew she needed to say something.

"No problem."

But there *was* a problem. She'd been rude to him and she didn't know how to bring it up without admitting that she'd known what she was doing at the time. "Mr. Santini…"

"Yeah?"

He stretched out the word like a piece of chewing gum. She hated to hear anyone using slang, but resisted the urge to correct him. "I want to apologize for my rude behavior when you were helping me out of the bathroom."

He stared at her until Cass was sure her hair must be standing on end or she had something on her face. She rubbed her nose before reaching into the stainless steel refrigerator to get the milk.

"I'm not used to a strange man being in my house."

"Then you shouldn't have sent your child out to find someone."

Cass stiffened. "I didn't send him to find someone. In fact I forbade him to leave, but Andy has a thing—" She broke off. Why would he care that Andy loved school and learning? Andy would go to any lengths to get to there.

"Well he didn't stay home. He came to my house. How the hell do you know I'm not an ax murderer, rapist or child molester?"

Cass sputtered, trying to figure out a way of defending what she knew was an indefensible position. Andy had gone before she could stop him. The boy was getting a bit impulsive, but that didn't excuse her for letting him go.

"You're right. I don't know anything about you, except—"

"Except that I have nice buns."

Oh, Lord, why had she ever mentioned that to her sister?

Usually Andy was involved with playing and didn't pay the least attention to her. But on that day, he'd obviously listened. She sought to change the conversation. "And a dog."

"Tundra?"

"We've seen you outside with her. Andy loves animals."

The coffeemaker spurted and spluttered, filling the silent kitchen with noise. Cass nervously glanced around the room, looking everywhere but at her rescuer.

"Mommy, I'm ready to go."

Andy stepped into the kitchen, wearing jeans and a G.I. Joe T-shirt. His new tennis shoes were spotless, but the laces were loosely tied.

"Come over here." She knelt next to him to fasten his shoes, grateful for the distraction. It reassured her that she and Andy had to leave soon, that she wouldn't have to stay and make small talk with Mr. Santini.

"There you go," she said, rising to her feet. "Grab your lunch bag, honey."

She poured coffee into two large foam cups, handing one to Mr. Santini and keeping the other for herself.

"Milk or sugar?" she asked.

He declined both. Andy grabbed a handful of oatmeal raisin cookies, offering a few to Mr. Santini, who took them.

"We're going to be late," Cass said. "Andy, did you close the upstairs windows?"

"No," he said. "I'll run—"

"I'll close the house up for you. Go on, get this little guy to school."

Cass hesitated for a moment, then remembered that Mr. Santini owned a reputable construction and land-development company. As president of the home owners' association, she'd approved his application for purchase. She knew more about Santini than she should. He was a respected member of the business community and a supporter of the Police Athletic League. There was really nothing in her house that he couldn't afford to buy for himself.

"Thanks," she said, herding Andy out the door. "That's two I owe you."

"Bye, Mr. Santini," Andy said, waving.

Cass backed the Volvo out of the drive, wondering how she was going to deal with her new neighbor and the debt that now stood between them. All the way to school Andy talked about Rafe Santini, and that worried her more than she wanted to admit.

She dropped Andy off in front of the school just as the bell rang. She watched him run toward his classroom on legs that were no longer chubby. Andy was beginning to lose that little boy look and becoming more like a young man. He was only seven years old, but looked a lot like his father, small and lean. Andy had come home from school with a black eye two weeks ago. Since then, he'd followed her dictate on "no fighting" but had ended up feeling insecure. Cass wasn't sure what to do with her son now.

She wished he would stay her baby forever but knew that wouldn't happen. Andy was getting too hard to handle, she thought with a sigh. She'd always believed that a child's upbringing would influence his actions, but Andy had a willful streak a mile wide. She hated to admit it, but she needed help with him.

Now she had a macho man with a swagger a mile wide living across the street. She thought about her new neighbor and how Andy had taken an instant liking to the man. Trouble was brewing.

She could cope now, but in a few years, if she didn't assert herself, Andy would be racing all over the place and getting into real trouble. Mr. Santini was no help at all. Running around in those skimpy jogging shorts of his every morning. He looked like every young boy's image of what a man should be. An athlete and a macho warrior rolled into one. It was enough to give a grown woman a heart attack.

Rafe drove a classic Jaguar sports car and probably dated women with big boobs and bleached blond hair. He was definitely not her type, and definitely not a good influence for a young boy.

But his earlier concern came back to her. He'd lit into her about letting Andy out of the house without supervision. She wondered if there was more to him than that bad-boy facade indicated. Did Rafe Santini care?

She pulled into her driveway and let the car idle for a minute before shutting it off. She hesitated to get out, reluctant to face her neighbor again. But at the same time, an edgy sort of nervousness made her limbs tingle and her pulse race.

She went into the house and filled her portable carafe with coffee before going across the street. Rafe sat on his front porch, his Siberian husky sprawled at his feet. Both were completely relaxed. Rafe's eyes were closed, and Cass stood there, staring at him.

"Oh, no," she muttered. "He's asleep."

One gray eye blinked open and glanced up at her. Cass cleared her throat and lifted her carafe. She leaned against the porch railing next to his lounge chair. "Want a refill?"

"Now that's right neighborly of you," he responded lazily, picking up his empty cup from the porch.

Silence settled around them, and Cass stifled the urge to run back to her own safe home. Her experience with men was limited to her late husband, Carl. She'd never had a chance to experiment with boys, having married right out of high school.

"Mr. Santini—"

"Rafe."

She nodded, but didn't use his name. "I have an offer for you."

He grinned. "Does it involve my buns?"

Cass blushed. She felt the heat of it radiating from her face. She was going to have to have a talk with Andy when he came home.

"No. It involves something else."

He raised one eyebrow at her, studying her with the intensity of a carpenter about to cut into mahogany.

"Well?"

"I wanted to um…" This was harder than she thought it would be. "I wanted to thank you for helping me out this morning and see if there was something I could do to repay you."

"Well, now that you mention it there is one thing I'd like."

His eyes narrowed and his gaze swept slowly down her body, sending signals to parts that had lain dormant for a long time. She fidgeted and stepped away from the railing and away from Mr. Santini.

"What do you want?"

"You," he said.

# Two

The teasing glint in Rafe's eyes kept Cass from making a fool of herself. She forced a smile to her lips and took a deep cleansing breath. Her pulse rate still hammered annoyingly high, making her feel like a schoolgirl. "I'm serious, Mr. Santini."

"Call me Rafe."

His eyes were truly remarkable. So light and clear in that dark, teasing face. She wondered if he was ever serious. But then she remembered his concern for Andy earlier this morning. Lurking beneath that carefree exterior was a man she could like, and that scared her.

"Okay...Rafe." His name felt strange on her tongue. If he'd been more like Tony, her brother-in-law, or the slightly balding Marcus, who lived down the street, it would have been so simple. She could have pretended he was a buddy.

But he wasn't. He was a dark-skinned Italian dream man with all the confidence in the world. Cass felt out of her depth with Rafe Santini. She swallowed hard. "I was more or less welcoming you to the neighborhood and offering to return the favor if you ever got locked in your bathroom."

He raised one eyebrow, clearly questioning her suggestion of repayment. His mouth quirked in a half grin that made her pulse race. "Won't Mr. Gambrel have something to say about that?"

Carl would have befriended any person who'd rescued her from the bathroom. He'd never been one of those jealous types. Steady, levelheaded and able to find the calm in chaos, her deceased husband had been an anchor. She still missed him, but at least she could say the words now without her throat closing up. "My husband is dead."

Rafe cursed under his breath.

The word was harsh and not one Cass had ever heard used by one of her peers. No man of her acquaintance used vulgarities. He reached out to her. One finger brushed against her arm, the texture of his work-roughened hands at odds with the gentleness in his tone.

"I'm sorry."

"It's okay." And it was. She'd come to terms with the loss of her husband a long time ago. Carl had been part of another life almost. But of course, he'd left her Andy. A constant and steady reminder of what they'd once shared.

There was something in Rafe's silver-gray eyes that mirrored the pain that she'd felt at Carl's loss—a pain that she'd recovered from. Somehow she thought that Rafe hadn't.

Who had he lost? She wanted to probe into his past and find out everything she could, but knew it would be an intrusion, to say nothing of unwise. Still, the sadness seemed at odds with what she'd observed about her new neighbor, and she couldn't help wondering about its source.

Cass knew little of Rafe's personal life. He'd moved into the neighborhood two weeks ago and she'd seen him only briefly when he'd been out jogging or playing with his dog.

Maybe it was better that way—having never met him, she'd felt safe fantasizing about him. Talking about him to Eve...

She should leave well enough alone, her common sense told her. But that sad, haunted look that had played briefly over his face wouldn't let her.

"I was hoping for an offer to clean the windows or the bathrooms," he said, a wicked grin on his face.

"No way," she retorted, fighting the urge to smile at him. He was a charming rascal, this Mr. Santini. "Call me if you're ever trapped in the bathroom or any other room in the house."

He balanced his coffee cup on his knee. His other hand rested absently on his chest, and for some reason Cass's eyes stared helplessly at it.

"Don't you have to go to work?" she asked abruptly, wondering why his lack of a shirt bothered her. Every other man on the street went without one in the summer. But it wasn't the same. She'd been raised that any decent person would never leave their house less than fully clothed, and finally she understood why.

He raised one eyebrow in a sardonic way. "I'm on vacation."

"Oh, got any plans?" she asked, hoping that he'd be leaving for Key West, Hawaii or Africa. Anywhere so that she would have time to adjust to being so attracted to him. Some part that had been dormant for a long time felt a tingle of life again. Why had she come over here this morning?

"Yes," he confirmed. "I'm making this house livable."

"Really? By yourself?" It had taken a crew of twenty men to finish the work on her house.

"My crew will be coming out at the end of the week to do the major overhaul. I'm going to finish the inside myself."

"You own a construction company, right?" Emily, her backyard neighbor, had told her all about Rafe Santini's business interests as soon as she'd found out he was moving into their neighborhood.

"RGS Construction and Development," he said with a touch of pride. His gaze slanted down over her. "Do you work?"

"Yes, I'm a mother, but I also run an antiques service from my home."

"What type of service?"

"I refinish antiques and help locate pieces that my clients need to complete a room."

"Sounds interesting. I'll keep you in mind when I start on the interior."

She glanced at his overgrown lawn, uncomfortable talking business with a neighbor. A change of subject was needed. "What's RGS stand for?"

"Raphael G. Santini." He took another sip of coffee. The dog stirred, then bounded off the porch to chase after a squirrel. Watching the dog in motion was a delight. She moved with the skill and cunning of a hunter. Cass suspected that Rafe would also move like a warrior.

Raphael, she thought, what a beautiful name. His mother must be a very romantic person to have come up with that. "What's the *G* stand for?"

"My middle name." He spoke in a sardonic way that made Cass think he saw life as one big joke.

"Very funny, Santini. Come on, confess. It can't be that bad." She walked closer, pinning him with her own version of the mother's stare. The one that always forced Andy to tell the truth.

"No way." He didn't sink back in the chair. The look on his face told her that he'd rather be tortured than admit his middle name. Interesting.

"I'm not intimidating you at all, am I?" she asked. Cass enjoyed Rafe's company as she hadn't enjoyed a man's in a long time.

"Nope." He smiled and sipped his coffee.

"Can I guess?" she asked.

"It's a free country."

"Is it George?"

He shook his head.

"Gary?"

Another negative response.

"Gregory?"

"Give it up, Ms. Gambrel. No one would guess the name in a million years."

"Call me Cass," she said without thinking.

He wasn't going to tell her, and she was honest enough to admit she didn't need to know. Cass then realized that she was hanging around his porch like some love-starved widow. She straightened away from the railing and prepared to leave. "See you around, Rafe."

"Thanks for the coffee, Cass."

A cheerful whistle followed her home, and Cass forbade herself to think of Rafe as anything but a neighbor. Well, possibly someone who could help her teach Andy discipline. But that was all.

"I'm not interested in Rafe Santini," she said out loud, hoping that saying the words would make them come true but even to her ears, the declaration sounded weak.

Damn that good-looking man and his cute backside. She added two cookies to the penalty of treats she couldn't have for using a curse word. At the rate she was going, she wouldn't be able to eat dessert until the year 2010.

Rafe worked on the roof all morning and into the afternoon. The tedious job of removing shingles left his mind free to wander. But it never went further than the lady across the street. A week had passed since he'd rescued her from the bathroom, and he still couldn't get the feel of her in his arms out of his mind.

And if he needed a further reminder, Andy was constantly underfoot, asking Rafe questions about every job he did. At first the boy had seemed annoying, and Rafe had been unsure what to say to the kid, but Andy was so serious. More of a miniadult than a child. That made talking to him easier.

Rafe always steered clear of "family" women. The type of lady looking for a man to be a husband and father to her kids. The type who wanted commitment. He didn't care for the way that word was bandied about on talk shows, but he knew it to be a goal of most females. A woman just wasn't happy until every bachelor she knew was married.

He liked being on his own, coming and going as he pleased and not having to answer to anyone. Loneliness didn't bother him anymore. His business was successful, and his life on track. He wasn't about to screw that up now by becoming attracted to a single mother.

His libido said differently, but Rafe felt firmly in control. He wasn't some sixteen-year-old virgin experiencing lust for the first time. He was a seasoned man. He was in control. "Ha," he muttered.

He climbed down off the roof and grabbed a beer from the cooler sitting on the porch. Maybe he'd hang the basketball hoop on the garage and see if he could entice anyone in the neighborhood into playing a game.

Hanging the hoop took all of fifteen minutes. Rafe finished off his beer with one long swallow and dug the orange ball out of a box in the garage. Walking back out onto the cement of the driveway, Rafe bounced the ball a couple of times.

"Hello, Mr. Santini." Andy Gambrel's shy voice broke his concentration. This serious little boy made Rafe want to go back inside. He was trying to forget Cassandra Gambrel, and her son was a reminder Rafe could have done without. They were a family and family meant pain. *Remember that.*

"Hi, Andy. How was school?"

A gap-toothed grin lit the boy's face. "Good. What are you doing?"

"Playing basketball. You up for a game?"

Andy glanced over his shoulder before nodding. Rafe

knew the boy was going against his mother's edict. "Have you ever played before?"

"No," he said. Andy shrugged, fidgeting from one foot to the other. He cast another glance over his shoulder at the house.

"Want to learn how?" Rafe asked. He had never met a child so serious. Andy seemed to be weighing the consequences of every decision he made.

At last he shook his head. "My mom says sports are for big brutes. Small guys like me were meant for the arts."

Rafe felt a spark of anger toward Cass. Sports helped boys develop into men. It gave them the training and discipline to see things through. Andy would need that discipline when he reached the teen years. Hell, the boy needed it now. Still, Rafe had no right to interfere.

"Well your mom's the boss, but if she changes her mind let me know." Rafe bounced the ball one more time before tossing it toward the hoop. It was a clean shot and didn't touch the rim.

"I've never really asked to play. I don't think Mom would mind if I threw the ball a time or two," Andy said.

Rafe figured the boy knew what he was doing. Dribbling the ball a few times, Rafe shot it toward the hoop, sinking the ball perfectly. Rafe passed the ball to Andy. "Your turn."

Andy tried, but his passes lacked the power to make a basket. The boy bounced the ball and kept glaring at the hoop as if it were his enemy. His shots were strong, but he missed sinking the shot every time.

"It's not your skill, Andy. The hoop's too high for someone your size."

"Mom was right then," he said, sounding unbearably forlorn.

"You need a lower hoop," Rafe said. "Or some help. Dribble the ball and I'll lift you when you're ready to dunk it."

Rafe heard the squeak of a screen door opening, but kept

his attention on Andy. He felt Cass's gaze on them. It took all of his discipline and willpower not to glance over his shoulder.

Andy bounced the ball a few times before he was ready for his shot. Rafe lifted him and together they made a basket. Andy's face glowed with the pride of success. "I did it! Wow, I can't believe it."

"Mommy, did you see that?" he asked turning to see her watching. Andy ran to her, hugging Cass's legs. "I can't believe it."

Rafe saw the conflict in Cass. Pride warred with anger and apprehension on her face. "Good job, sweetie, but you know the rule about sports."

"This was supervised."

Cass shook her head. "Okay, Andy, but next time I want you to ask for permission first."

"Thanks, Mommy."

"Go inside and wash up for dinner."

He left without another word. Rafe half hoped that he'd be dismissed also. But the gleam in Cass's eyes told him differently.

"Rafe, I don't like Andy playing sports. He's small for his age and I don't want him to get hurt."

"We weren't playing tackle football, just shooting some hoops."

"I know I'm overreacting. It's just that I'm not sure Andy's ready to get involved in sports. He's only seven."

"He'll be okay. He knows your rules, Cass."

She nodded, then straightened her shoulders as though preparing for an assault. "I'm the president of the Hollow Acres Home Owners' Association."

"Really? Must be some job."

"It doesn't take much time," she said, staring over his shoulder for a minute before meeting his gaze squarely. "That hoop is against our regulations."

"What?" he asked. Her ginger-colored eyes were serious now, but some of her earlier fear for Andy lingered.

"I'm issuing you a warning. You have two days to remove the hoop or you'll be fined."

"You're kidding, right?"

"Wrong, Mr. Santini, I'm serious about this." She reached down to scratch Tundra under her chin, and the dog's tongue lolled out of her mouth as she rolled onto her back. "Didn't you read the Owner's Agreement?"

He hadn't, but he couldn't think beyond the long legs revealed by her shorts. The fabric slid up her thigh as she bent to pet Tundra. He knew that she was in shape, but hadn't guessed at the muscle tone she had. Her legs were long and lean and he wanted to feel them wrapped around his waist.

Tension ripped through him, making a mockery of his control. Dammit, what had they been talking about? The Owner's Agreement. "How long has this agreement been in effect?"

"Since 1983 when the county commissioners asked us to make our houses uniform." She stood up and started to walk away.

"Well, maybe it's time we updated the rules."

She stopped and glanced back over her shoulder. "Maybe, but until we do, that hoop has to come down."

"What if it doesn't?" he asked to keep her there.

"Then you'll be fined," she said. She started back across the street. "Have a good night, Mr. Santini."

"You too, Cass."

Damn that woman. Underneath that prim and proper exterior lurked a temptress. A woman who liked to laugh and tease. He wanted to see more of that lady, he decided.

Cass held the phone against her shoulder and secured the leftover dinner in plastic wrap. Closing the refrigerator door with her hip as she started the dishes, she said, "I'll stop by first thing in the morning, Dana."

Cass thought about her friend and co-chair for the PTA

bake sale. Dana's son Jeff was in Andy's class, but the two boys didn't get along.

She hung up and stared out the window. Dusk had deepened into night, and the imitation gas street lamps were sparking to life. She liked this quiet neighborhood with its old houses.

Andy sat on the front porch doing his homework, and Cass quickly finished the dishes before joining her son. He had wanted to invite Mr. Santini to dinner, but Cass had put Andy off. Rafe's influence over Andy was getting out of hand.

Rafe didn't encourage Andy, but her son was hungry for masculine attention. The other day Andy had used a swearword that her son knew warranted strict punishment. She'd also seen her son leaving his shirt off and swaggering when he walked. The same way Mr. Santini did.

Rafe had included Andy in a softball game the previous Saturday. Her son was still talking about it and asking her every evening when he could join Little League football or baseball. Andy was obsessed with getting involved in sports and mimicking their new neighbor. Cass knew she had to put a stop to things and quickly.

The loud barking of Tundra announced the arrival of Rafe before he rounded the corner. Cass told herself not to look. That he was a temptation in those ridiculously skimpy running shorts, but her gaze was drawn to him all the same. If Rafe was an example of how men could look by running a few miles every night, men across America would be hitting the streets.

Cass pretended she didn't notice Rafe. He waved to Andy as he jogged up the walk. Tundra breathed heavily at his feet. Andy set his pencil aside and gave her a pointed look. "Mommy?"

Andy never phrased out questions when just a word or a look would get the point across. She debated for a moment and decided that the husky wouldn't hurt her son. She nodded slightly and Andy beamed with pleasure.

"Can I play with Tundra, Mr. Santini?"

"Sure," Rafe sat down on the bottom step as Andy bounded off the porch.

Cass watched her son toss a stick to the dog, and soon the animal and boy were playing on the lawn. "Would you like something cool to drink?"

"Got any beer?" he asked. He smelled of sweat and male muskiness. Cass wanted to lean closer to him, to feel him surrounding her, to inhale the scent that was subtly Rafe. She wanted to taste the sweat that glistened on his arm and to experience this man in a way that she'd thought she'd forgotten.

"No. Iced tea would be better for you." She couldn't help the way she'd been raised, and drinking except at family celebrations and holidays was strictly forbidden.

"Not if it's sugary."

Always a comeback, she thought, enjoying the game as much as he did. "Like beer has any nutritional value."

"What it lacks in nutrition it makes up for in taste."

He had to be kidding, beer tasted like...well like beer, nothing else even came close to that taste. "My tea's not sweet."

"Than I'll take you up on that offer."

She fixed them both a glass of tea before returning. This would be a good time to ask him to stop including Andy in games. There were a few man-type things that she didn't know how to handle, and this was one of them. How did you politely tell a man that he wasn't the right type of influence on your son?

Quite honestly there were more than a few things she didn't know about raising a son. Teaching Andy to color in the lines and to use the potty was easy compared to coaching him on ignoring bullies. She didn't want Andy to grow up being afraid of other boys, but at the same time she wanted him to be someone who used his mind to settle arguments, not his fists.

"Thanks," Rafe said as she sat down next to him on the step.

"You're welcome," she replied, trying to ignore the heat radiating from his body.

He took a long swallow of tea and then bounded to his feet. "Hey, Andy. Have you got a football around here?"

The boy shook his head. "Why?"

"Basketball is against the rules. I thought we could toss the pigskin around."

"Mommy?"

"If Mr. Santini has a ball than I don't object to your catching it," she reluctantly agreed. Tossing a ball wasn't the same as playing in a game, she reassured herself.

"As it happens, I do," Rafe said, grinning at her.

"All right!" Andy dropped the stick he'd been tossing to the dog and followed Rafe across the street.

Santini had been in their lives for only a short time, but already he had a lot of influence over Andy. She watched her son staring up at Rafe and wondered how a man who spent most of his time with beautiful women and fast cars would react to blind hero worship.

She started to call Andy back, but Rafe was showing him how to hold the football. Cass watched her little boy come one day closer to manhood, and a part of her wanted to die. She'd carefully guarded Andy, but she had the feeling that soon he would throw off that protection.

Rafe helped Andy the way a father would help a son. Showing him things that only a man could. Cass felt convinced that Andy was becoming too attached to their neighbor. Her son was using Mr. Santini as fill-in father.

She couldn't picture Rafe in the role of a dad. He treated Andy kindly, but sometimes he acted as if her son were an alien being. Having Andy underfoot had to be trying for a man like Rafe.

Cass watched them playing ball in the front yard and forgot that Rafe wasn't the fatherly type. He seemed perfectly at ease with her son for perhaps the first time since they'd met. She couldn't believe this was the same man who roared out of the neighborhood once a day in his Jaguar convertible.

Her heart ached as she watched them playing ball. She wanted the scene to be real. She needed a man to share her life and Andy's. She knew that Rafe wasn't that man but it was still hard to stop her heart from hoping.

She went inside to prepare a snack for Rafe and Andy, knowing they'd be hungry when the game wrapped up. There was something homey about preparing iced tea for two sweaty males, Cass thought with a smile. Tundra snoozed under the oak in the front yard and Cass felt content for the first time in years.

# Three

Rafe tossed the football to Andy and watched the kid jump to catch the ball. The boy had the potential to be a dedicated athlete. The desire to succeed burned brightly in his eyes. He had the innate skill that few possessed and seemed to enjoy every sport that Rafe introduced to him. The grin on Andy's face erased much of the apprehension Rafe usually felt when dealing with the boy.

Rafe hadn't been around children for the majority of his life. In fact the last time he'd been with other kids was— he searched his memories—hell, not since he was a boy.

Kids were foreign entities that Rafe didn't deal well with. They were crying, sticky little people that always talked loudly. But Andy Gambrel was different. Andy had a sense of maturity seldom found in one so young.

The other kids in the neighborhood were older than Andy, and Rafe had watched the boy playing alone over the last week. Something about the solitary way the boy had amused himself generated a sort of sympathy in Rafe.

No child should be left to himself like that. Rafe never had been, and for some reason he didn't want Cass's son to be, either.

Andy tossed the ball back to him, and Rafe caught it one-handed. "Have you ever gone to a basketball game, Andy?"

"No, we've been down to the Bob Carr auditorium for plays and musicals though." Andy scrunched his face in a look of pain. "Sometimes we see people going to the Magic games."

"What show did you see?"

"A French play *Les Misérables*," Andy said, correctly pronouncing the French title. "It was okay for the first twenty minutes, but all that singing was boring. Mommy really liked it. She even cried."

Rafe chuckled.

"I bet the Orena—the Orlando Arena—is great."

The touch of envy in the boy's voice was barely audible, but there. Rafe wondered if Cass realized how much her son wanted to go to a game. Probably not, or she would have taken him. She was a good and caring mother, even if she was a bit overprotective.

"Have you seen the Magic play?"

"Yeah," Rafe said. "I have season tickets."

"Oh," the boy said, so softly and wistfully that Rafe bit back a grin. The kid wasn't stupid and had an understanding of manipulation that would have made any father proud.

They tossed the ball back and forth a few more times. "You want to go to a game sometime?"

"Wow, I'd love to. But Mom would never let me go. She's still ticked about the softball game last weekend."

Cass had to loosen up. Her son was starting to develop into a man, and she was fighting him every step of the way. "What's wrong with the softball game?"

"I wasn't exactly honest about what we were doing," Andy confessed.

"We'll see if she wants to go with us," Rafe suggested.

"You think she might want to?" Andy asked.

No, Rafe figured she wouldn't want to go, but saying no to her son was going to be hard. "It can't hurt to ask."

They rejoined Cass who brought out more iced tea and freshly baked bran muffins. Cass reminded him of every ideal that American men had about a mother. She was kind, firm and caring. She baked, cleaned and was at home when Andy arrived from school.

At the same time she had a sexy little body that made Rafe think of long hours spent in bed. That was why he kept coming back. Why he put up with her lectures on using correct grammar and not cussing. She was Rafe's ideal of the perfect woman, which is why he would never allow himself to have a relationship with her. No man would ever have just a fling with her. She was the kind of woman a man made a commitment to. A commitment was the one thing he couldn't offer her.

"Cass, I asked Andy to join me at a Magic game tomorrow night, and I'd like for you to come with us. What do you say?"

Her gingery eyes widened with speculation, and he saw the refusal written there before she opened her mouth. "Thank you for asking, but Andy and I wouldn't be able to find tickets to the game. I hear they're sold out."

Tricky lady. She always had an excuse handy, but this time he was prepared. "I have season tickets."

She glanced at her son, and Rafe could see her weighing the consequences of declining. She sighed, and it was not a welcoming sound. "Well, then I guess we'd be happy to go with you."

Cass spent the morning pretending not to notice Rafe. Andy had talked about the impending basketball game all the way to school. She had the feeling that this was going to win her son a lot of points with his friends. Not many second-graders were invited to go to see the Orlando Magic play.

Cass sighed. By nature she was calm and unflappable, but Rafe Santini had a way of making her forget to be calm and unflappable. He'd put several wood cutouts across the front of his lawn of a woman bent at the waist with her frilly drawers showing. In front of his porch he'd placed large, plastic flowers in florescent blue, orange and green. He had the most hideous looking yard on the street.

The complete craziness of the yard was at odds with the man who patiently taught her son to play catch and the finer points of basketball. This was the man who wanted to needle her because she made him remove his basketball hoop.

Rafe's multidimensional personality kept her on her toes. The sexy man made her nervous and achy in places that she hadn't thought of in a long time—secure emotional places that she'd forgotten. He made her feel vulnerable, and that wasn't necessarily bad because Rafe also made her laugh again.

She liked his sense of humor, which was almost always present. She liked the deep well of patience he showed with Andy. And most of all she liked the way he dug in and finished a job no matter how dirty or tedious. She just plain liked him and that *was* dangerous.

He worked on his house in denim cutoffs that should have been illegal. The faded material clung to his legs, revealing every muscular inch. His backside had originally drawn her attention, and she stared at him now as he hefted a box of shingles onto his shoulder.

He sang a lively country tune about trashy women and bopped along to the music. He had his own style, she thought with a grin. If one could call it style. She giggled out loud, picturing Rafe in one of the trendy men's magazines.

As usual he wore no shirt, though she tried not to notice. Why couldn't he have a paunch around the middle? Or a soft belly and flabby legs? Was that too much to ask?

She watched his muscles ripple with each movement of

the hammer. Cass stared at his back until she realized what she was doing. Get a grip, girl, she admonished herself.

Rafe waved at her, and Cass knew she'd been caught staring up at him. She raised her hand in acknowledgment, and he just grinned in a way that made her want to run in the house and hide.

Cass forced her attention back to the Victorian Renaissance chair she was reupholstering for Mrs. Parsons. Rafe's decadent image haunted her. She hated to think she was turning into a slavering sex fiend, but the man refused to stay out of her mind and his naked chest wasn't helping.

The hammering stopped, and Cass scowled as she glanced up again. Rafe worked on a two-man job by himself. He rolled out the tar paper and hammered in the tacks before starting the process all over. At the rate he labored, the small section he was reroofing might not be finished until tonight.

Cass finished adding the trim to the chair, then stood and brushed the fabric threads off her khaki shorts. Her mother had raised her to be neighborly, and that meant offering help. She crossed the quiet street and shielded her eyes against the sun.

"Hello, Santini." She wanted to put distance between them, and using his last name helped her to think of him as a buddy.

Rafe finished securing the section he was working on before glancing down at her. "Morning, Gambrel."

That he didn't mention her earlier gawking earned him points for tact, which she honestly admitted she'd thought he lacked.

She wished she'd changed into jeans before coming over. For some reason Rafe seemed to be glaring at her legs. Cass was generally happy about the way she looked, but now she thought about the extra five pounds she hadn't lost since Christmas last year. "Do you need some help?"

"No," he said, and rolled out another section of tar paper. "I roof in my sleep."

Feeling put in her place, she wanted to escape. Her conscience demanded she make one more offer of help. "Wouldn't two hands make the job go faster?"

"Yeah, I guess it would." He sat back on his heels. "You're not feeling guilty, are you?"

The twinkle in his eye warned her he was up to no good. But like an unsuspecting mackerel being lured to a fisherman's hook, she swallowed the bait. "Guilty about what?"

"Sitting under the shade of the porch while I labored out in the hot sun."

"Santini, don't you know better than to give the help a hard time?" she asked before walking back toward her house.

"I guess not, Gambrel."

She stopped and glanced over her shoulder. "Should I stay?"

"Yes, ma'am, please."

The polite tone to his words made her think he might be teasing again. She took a step toward the ladder intending to climb up to the roof. "Hang loose, Gambrel. I'll be right down."

In a matter of minutes Rafe was at her side. "You'll need a tool belt and a hammer."

"I thought I'd just hand you things and hold them in place." She really didn't know that much about home repair.

"What *things*, Cass?" He poured roofing tacks into one of the pockets on the leather tool belt.

"Nails and stuff." She fidgeted, shifting her weight from one foot to the other.

"You're a real tools expert." But there was no censure in his tone, only the teasing lilt she'd come to expect.

"You're treading on thin ice, Santini," she warned him, playing along with his game.

"I'm scared, Gambrel. Real scared." He handed her a rubber-handled hammer. "Turn around."

She did and was engulfed by Rafe. His body warmth and

musky scent surrounded her as he wrapped the tool belt around her waist and fastened it. If she leaned back an inch she'd be pressed up against his chest. A shiver passed through her, and temptation warred with good sense as she thought of his naked chest.

"There you go," he said. His voice sounded different. A deeper, huskier version of his usual tone that made her aware of the difference between them. He stepped away from her and put his hand on her shoulders, turning her to face him.

"Thanks," she managed to squeeze out of her dry throat. The weight around her was unaccustomed and felt weird.

Cass settled the hammer into one of the loops. Rafe passed her a scraper and a few other tools she couldn't identify. "Is that all?"

"Distribute the weight of the hammer and the mallet."

She moved the tools around. Well, she felt downright handy now.

"Do those shoes have good soles?"

"Yes, I think so."

He knelt down near her knees. "Let me take a look at the bottom of your shoes."

His breath brushed across her thigh and the muscle quivered. He was so close. Cass's fingers itched with the urge to bury themselves in his thick black hair.

Cass swayed and her leg scraped against his cheek. The stubbly texture of his skin felt good against the smoothness of her own. Thank heavens she'd shaved her legs yesterday. She leaned away from him in embarrassment. He probably thought she was a love-starved widow.

"Put your hand on my shoulder for balance."

His words were harsh, almost guttural. Cass knew their brief encounter had affected Rafe as much as it had affected her. She hoped it had. Her heart was beating loud enough to be heard a mile a way.

Oh, damn. She didn't want this headlong rush into desire. Not now when her life was finally starting to balance out.

She was independent and in charge of her own life, but a part of her still longed for someone to hold in the middle of the night. Not just anyone, but a certain man who could fill the emptiness inside of her.

Her hand rested on the tightly corded muscles of his shoulder as he examined the bottom of her shoes. He straightened and gave her the once-over. "Okay, you're ready to work."

They labored on the roof for the next two hours. Cass found roofing a hard but interesting task. They'd almost completed the section by mid-afternoon, and she was relieved to know that she'd helped Rafe.

The sun was hot and Cass felt her face begin to pinken. "I need a break."

Rafe glanced over at her. "You sure do. Go sit over there in the shade."

A large maple tree provided shade on the east side of the roof. Walk across the roof by herself? No way. "I'll stay right here."

"Scared, Gambrel?"

Cass wasn't the type to take a dare. She freely admitted to her faults. And she wasn't going to pretend to be someone she wasn't. She doubted that this strong man ever did. "Yes, I am."

He reached out and brushed a finger across her cheek. "There's no need to be. I won't let you fall."

But she was afraid that he would. Not fall off the roof. Rafe was too good a crew boss to allow any of his workers to get physically injured. But with each minute she spent with this man a part of her trod deeper into dangerous territory. Emotional territory that could spell trouble for her. Territory she hadn't explored since the early days of her marriage.

He offered her his hand and seated her in the shade before retrieving two cans of fruit punch from an ice chest. He walked with the surety of a cat...no a streetwise warrior. Someone who knew that he could take on any situation. Cass envied him his confidence.

She'd felt weak and shaky most of her life. First with the loss of her father when she was sixteen, then with the loss of Carl when she was twenty-six. Instinctively she was drawn to strong men, yet a part of her resented their strength.

He was watching her, and that made her nervous. She took a long sip of the punch. The sweet liquid left an aftertaste and she set the can aside. "I'd like to invite you to dinner before we leave for the game tonight."

"It would be easier to grab something at the Orena."

Cass digested that. "Were you able to purchase tickets for us?"

"I told you I have season tickets." He stared at her for a full minute before continuing. "Why didn't you want Andy to go alone with me?"

Cass hedged for a moment. Short of out and out lying, there was no way to avoid the truth. "I don't like the enthusiasm you have for sports. Andy looks up to you. What you do, he wants to do, and he's so small for his age, I'm afraid he'll get hurt."

"Watching a game?"

"You know that once he gets the bug for any game he'll be hooked, and then I'll seem like an ogre if I don't let him participate."

"Cass, I'm not trying to influence your son. I thought the game sounded like a good idea, but if you didn't want him to go, you should have just said no."

"I know, but Andy wants to get involved in some after-school activities, and I wanted to ask for your help with something."

He stared at the top of the aluminum can. "I have no experience with kids, Cass."

"I know. This is kind of a-man-who-was-once-a-boy question."

He grinned. "Well, I *was* a boy once."

"Somehow I suspected you might have been," she said before blurting out, "Andy asked me to let him join peewee football."

"That's up to you," Rafe said. Cass knew he didn't want to be caught up in their lives.

"Rafe, I don't want Andy to grow up being a little wimp because I never let him try things. But I also don't want him to get hurt, and football is dangerous. I've heard tales from other mothers in the PTA."

His light eyes were piercing in their intensity. "Injuries happen, Cass. But participating in a sport helps develop discipline."

Silently Cass heard the censure from their first meeting. Discipline was something Andy lacked. Her son ran wild when he wanted to, and Cass knew she was to blame. "Can you suggest an alternative to football?"

"Let me think about it." He stood up before tugging her to her feet. "You need to get out of the sun for a while."

"What's that mean?"

"You're turning pink, lady."

She ran her eyes over his almost bare body. His olive skin had merely deepened in the late-October sun, but if she stayed out much longer she'd look like a lobster. "I'm going."

She held tightly to Rafe's fingers as he led her across the steep roof to the ladder. She glanced down before taking her first step onto the aluminum ladder and felt the world tip on its axis. She closed her eyes as dizziness swamped her.

"I think I'll stay up here for a while longer." Maybe the rest of her natural life. She could watch Andy grow up from the roof.

"Come on, little coward. I'll help you down."

She stiffened and drew away from Rafe, but didn't release his hand. "I'm not a coward. Anyone with common sense would be wary of falling."

"I know, Cass," he said in the gentlest tone of voice she'd ever heard him use. "I'll go down first."

Rafe surrounded her completely as they descended. She should have felt only cherished, safe and protected. But she also felt the first dangerous spark of passion. Her nipples tightened against the lace of her bra, and her body ached.

She leaned into Rafe's chest and stopped climbing down. He paused, too, a harsh groan coming from his throat, and he rubbed his chest against her back.

"Rafe?" she asked, not sure what she wanted or what she was asking for. Only that she would regret that "something" if she never experienced it. Rafe made her feel alive. Like a woman who'd been frozen for a long time and was only now encountering her true self.

His lips brushed the nape of her neck, and electric shivers coursed through her body. He was warm and hard behind her, and she felt as safe as she would have, flat on the ground. She sank back against him, wanting more than this time and place could offer them.

"Cassie," he murmured as he ran his lips along the length of her neck. His hands were still secured around her waist, but she'd felt his fingers making forays toward the bottom of her breasts.

Tundra barked loudly, breaking the moment as nothing else could have. Cass felt her face heat with a blush of shame. What could she have been thinking to react so shamelessly in a man's arms? Especially this very experienced man's. This man who had women at his beck and call and who was more worldly than Cass would ever want to be.

Rafe was moving again. In a moment they were safely on the ground. "Cass, you okay?"

His voice was sincere and kind and, dammit, she hated how weak and vulnerable she felt. "I'm fine. See you tonight."

Cass left before he asked questions she didn't want to answer. She was achy and shaking when she entered her air-conditioned house. She had a bad case of lust for a totally inappropriate man. What the heck was she going to do?

Rafe always wore jeans and a Magic shirt to all the games he attended. He figured Cass wouldn't have thought to buy herself and Andy one, so he brought shirts for them. He looked forward to showing Cass part of his world.

Rafe also anticipated his good-night kiss. There was no question that he was going to claim one. Her mouth was tempting the hell out of him, and tonight he would know the feel of it under his own. He would know the feel of her in his arms.

Introducing Cass to sports had the side benefit of helping little Andy convince his mom that participating in a game was okay. Though Rafe cautioned himself against caring for the little boy, he liked the kid.

Rafe froze as it suddenly hit him that he was involving himself in this family's life. He'd sworn not to let himself care for anyone after the death of his family, and he'd lived up to that until now. Until Cass Gambrel had tempted him to care. But along with the temptation was a niggling sense of warning. Mama, Papa and Angelica had depended on him, and he'd let them down. Firmly pushing the faces of the past out of his mind's eye, he knocked on the door and heard running footsteps on the stairs.

"I've got it."

Rafe grinned. Andy was a lovable kid.

"Hi, Mr. Santini. I thought you'd never get here."

Rafe handed one of the T-shirts to Andy.

"Wow, thanks, Mr. Santini. Mommy, he's here," the boy yelled up the stairs.

"I know, sweetie," Cass said from the top of the stairs.

She looked as he imagined she would. Casual, comfortable and chic. Not that she would think of herself in those terms. She wore a light green polo shirt and khaki pants.

Rafe was counting on Andy's help to get Cass to change

into jeans and the T-shirt he'd brought for her. "You look nice, but I brought you a shirt to wear tonight."

Cass walked carefully down the stairs, stopping next to Rafe. He held up the shirt, measuring it against her. He'd gotten the smallest size available, but he had a feeling it would still be too big on her.

"I don't know. I look funny in T-shirts."

"Please, Mommy," Andy cajoled without any prompting from Rafe.

"Come on, Cass. Everyone wears them."

"Okay, I'll go change."

Twenty minutes later they were on their way. Rafe drove Cass's Volvo through the downtown traffic. Andy sat in the backseat and talked about everything under the sun from school to television then back to school again.

Rafe tried to concentrate on the traffic and driving, but the image of Cass as she'd looked coming down the stairs was burned on his brain. Her jeans were time-worn and faded, hugging every feminine curve tightly. He'd had to ball his hands into fists to keep from reaching out and caressing her sweet rear end.

The T-shirt had draped over her curves and clung to her breasts when she'd put on her jacket. For a moment lust had hit him so hard that he couldn't breath. He'd stood there, rooted to the spot, staring at her.

Finally they arrived at the arena. Cass held tightly to Andy's hand, which the little boy tolerated for only a few minutes without complaint. "Mommy, let go. I'll stand right next to you."

"No, Andrew. There are too many cars out here tonight."

Rafe knew they were heading toward a major mother-son argument and did the only thing he could think of to forestall it. "I'll hold your Mom's hand, too. How's that sound?"

Andy nodded, and Cass looked apprehensive. Rafe took

her hand on the side closest to the road and leaned down. "I won't bite you."

"I didn't think you would."

He laughed as they walked up the stairs leading to the entrance. Cass made him feel good in a way that he hadn't in a long, long time.

Throughout the game Andy had cheered like the Magic's number-one fan. During time-outs and the game breaks, he'd put the pressure on Cass to let him participate in a sport. Cass gently but firmly told the boy no each time.

When one of the players was injured, she looked at Rafe and Andy without saying a word. Rafe understood what she was trying to convey. Her baby wanted to play a game that could hurt him, and as long as there was a breath in her body Cass would worry about him.

Rafe drove down their street and pulled into Cass's driveway. He glanced into the backseat and saw Andy curled on his side fast asleep. Rafe realized he didn't want to see the boy hurt, either.

But the rational part of his mind knew that for every person injured in a sport, a dozen kids were never hurt. He wondered if he should try to convince Cass of that. *Don't get involved,* his inner voice cautioned.

"Want me to carry him up for you?" Rafe asked when he'd turned the car off.

"Please." Cass opened the front door, and Rafe followed her to Andy's bedroom. He set the boy on the bed and stood in the doorway watching as Cass changed Andy into his pajama's. He felt a tugging at his heart and left the bedroom.

Ah, hell, this wasn't supposed to happen. A woman with a family and that long chain called "commitment" wasn't supposed to make him feel this way. Lust was easy to handle, but what he felt for Cass was more intense.

He was Rafe Santini. A loner, a hard worker and, most importantly, a man with no emotional ties. He repeated the words like a mantra on his way down the stairs, but he couldn't get Cass out of his mind.

The night sky beckoned, and Cass stared up at the stars glittering in the distance. Rafe's voice had a soothing effect on her, making her feel drowsy. The wine wasn't helping, she thought, setting her glass aside.

She'd never drunk alcohol without a reason before. Rafe's influence had spilled over from Andy to her, corrupting years of teachings. Cass admitted to herself that it felt good to be doing something different, something a little bit daring.

"Basketball is one of the safest sports out there," Rafe said, pushing the swing into motion. His arm lay against the back of the seat, and Cass fought the impulse to lean against him. His warmth, his scent, her own naughty thoughts urged her to scoot closer.

Rafe was silent, waiting for her to say something. What had he said? Something about basketball. She forced herself to pay attention to the conversation. She smiled at Rafe and made a vague reply.

Debating the merits of basketball helped her to vocalize all of her arguments. Rafe was well versed in sports and was frank in his reasoning. Instead of glossing over the disadvantages as she'd expected him to, Rafe discussed them clearly. He wanted to help her make the right choice, and Cass knew that it was difficult for him.

She pretended she didn't care about Rafe, but knew that wasn't true. "Thanks for taking us to the game tonight."

"You're welcome. I hope that I didn't encourage Andy in the wrong way." His eyes seemed to glow with the faint light spilling from the kitchen window. Rafe always put on a tough act, and Cass admitted that at first she didn't even try to see past his facade, but now she saw the caring man underneath.

In a short time her little family had started to care about the man across the street. Tonight he'd proven that he could be part of their family, yet she knew that he didn't want to. Every time Andy had grabbed his hand to share the excitement over a play, Rafe had pulled away.

Cass took a sip of her wine, then glanced over at Rafe. "Did you play basketball when you were a boy?"

"Yes, I did. I participated in every sport available. My mom hated it at first, but eventually she came to accept it."

In that moment she knew she more than cared for Rafe, that some part of her would always want to be near him, even if she were nothing more than a friend. This man had a wealth of emotions bottled up inside of him, and he never let them out.

Why do you care, she asked herself, and refused to answer. She reached out, running her fingertip along his stubbly jaw. He felt wonderful and masculine, and she wanted nothing more than to kiss him. She needed to meet Rafe on an intimate level—a level new to her.

She didn't have the experience to know how to entice a man, but thinking about their earlier encounter on the ladder bolstered her confidence. Carl had always been the aggressor in their marriage, and frankly, she'd never felt this intensely about her deceased husband.

Her stomach was full of butterflies; she knew she needed to feel Rafe's arms wrapped around her. She glanced into his silver eyes and froze. Rafe stared at her with a hunger she'd never seen in a man's eyes before—at least not directed at her.

He cursed softly and rested his forearms on spread knees. "I'm not the kind of man who'd be a good influence on kids."

"I'm not asking you to be," she said, and meant it. Right now she only wanted to feel his arms around her, his lips on hers, and to experience Rafe in a very elemental way.

He faced her, and Cass felt the light of hope die. "You're a commitment, Cass, and I'm not ready for that."

Rafe's sincerity touched her as few things in life ever had. She reached out to touch him, needing, in that moment, to feel the warmth of his skin. "I only want a friend, Rafe."

He raised one eyebrow in question in the quirky way she'd come to love.

"It's true. Friendship is all I want or have time for."

"We can't be friends."

"Then kiss me goodbye and I'll never bother you again." Cass couldn't believe she'd said that, but dammit, part of her would die if she didn't experience his kiss just once.

"Cassie, you don't know what you do to me," he muttered. He set his wineglass on the porch and took hers from her hand. "Come here, baby. I'll kiss you, but it won't be goodbye."

# Four

**K**issing Cassandra was like coming home after a long journey. Cautioning himself to move slowly and not overwhelm Cass was harder than it sounded. He was bombarded with strange new emotions and a feeling of intimacy that Rafe had never experienced before.

It had been years since anyone had slipped past his barriers. He wasn't sure he liked the feeling. He had forgotten how a rush of caring could swamp his senses. Everything happened at once, leaving his head spinning.

Rafe knew he shouldn't be kissing her. Cassandra Gambrel threatened his easy-living life-style and his mental sanity. Questions sprang to life, but were quickly suppressed again as desire started his blood roiling. God, she felt right in his arms. He tightened his embrace.

Sweet-smelling jasmine surrounded them, filling the night air with its seductive fragrance. Cass's slenderness, her fragility, had never seemed so apparent as when he held her close to his side. Her lips opened under his in complete surrender. She moaned at the first contact of tongue on tongue. Rafe stifled his own sigh.

He sipped at her mouth, addicted to the sweetness of her. She tasted faintly of wine and another, more subtle, flavor. He tasted her again and again until he placed it as the spearmint gum she'd been chewing earlier.

Cass's hair was softer than a mink coat under his fingers, sliding across his palm like a cool breeze off the ocean. An empty part of his soul cried out for more of her, and he indulged himself in the feel of Cassandra. Rafe supported her neck, bending over her and deepening their embrace.

He thrust his tongue into the honeyed warmth of her mouth. He wanted all of her...now. He wanted her out of the T-shirt and jeans. He wanted to feel the tender skin of her body, to taste it with his mouth, to caress it with his fingers, to make love to her with his body and, though he hated to admit it, his soul. He wanted her long, slim legs wrapped around his waist as he pounded out the demanding rhythm pumping through his veins.

Her fingers on his neck and shoulders felt like a warm ray of sunshine. Rafe groaned in frustration, knowing that for Cass this embrace would have to stop here. It couldn't be followed to its natural conclusion, because Cass wasn't the type of woman who would sleep with a man on the first date.

Her soft breasts brushed against his chest as she snuggled closer to him. Cass's arms encircled his neck, her fingers grasping in his hair. He pulled his mouth from hers, trailing kisses down her cheek to her neck.

Cass tightened her grip on his shoulders, lowering her head to meet his. She sought his lips with hers and nibbled gently before she kissed him. At first just a tentative tasting, but then with building passion.

She shifted until her body was pressed against his. Rafe rubbed his chest to hers, glorying in the contact and the knowledge that he could make her react to him in this way.

She moaned and moved against him with abandon. Desire quickened his blood, and his body stirred to readiness. He wanted her now. And he would take her if he kept on this way.

Years of experience had given him intimate knowledge of a woman's body and the skill to use that knowledge expertly. He could make her body want his so badly that years of scruples and morals wouldn't stand a chance.

Sickened at the thought, Rafe pushed Cass away. He stood and turned from her. Placing both hands on the front porch railing, he breathed deeply. He forced himself to count to a hundred before even thinking about Cass again. His lungs felt as if they would burst with the air he pulled in, but he kept up the exercise, refusing to turn and look at Cass.

"Rafe?"

The trembling voice that called his name made his heart clench. He refused to look back at her, knowing that if he did, his good intentions would be shot to hell. He was that far gone. Control was a distant memory when faced with this woman. Dammit, he cursed silently. Why hadn't he left well enough alone? Why had he kissed her?

But he knew he'd had no choice. He'd kissed Cassandra Gambrel because he couldn't *not* kiss her. For days he'd been thinking about those soft lips that were almost, but not quite, pink. He'd thought about the slender body and the way she moved with an unconscious gracefulness that was extremely seductive. He'd thought about her legs, which were never completely bare, but oh, so long that his imagination went wild thinking about them wrapped around—

"Rafe?"

Her voice sounded vulnerable, scared and a bit unsure. Rafe had always dated women who knew the score. Cass didn't. She was as far removed from his life-style as Jupiter was from the Sun.

Why should the first woman to make him feel alive in ages be the one woman he couldn't have? *And he couldn't have her.* He knew it with bone-deep certainty and accepted it the way he accepted that his parents were dead. The way he accepted that he'd never again experience a sense of family and belonging. The way he'd accepted how his own lack of control had brought their deaths.

He straightened and glanced over at her. She sat, huddled into herself like a wounded mouse. Rafe felt like a big bird of prey that had stalked and injured the mouse, but wouldn't finish the kill. The feeling wasn't a new one. He'd felt it during the long hours he'd sat by Angelica's bedside and willed her to live.

He strode off the porch without a word, knowing he was the world's biggest bastard. He wondered how he'd ever be able to face her gingery eyes again without seeing them bright with tears and filled with a hurt he'd caused.

Cass knocked on the heavy oak door and waited with dread for Rafe to appear. This morning she'd tried every excuse she could think of to avoid coming over to his house, but three other board members had called about his yard. The lawn decorations had to go, and the grass needed to be mowed.

She felt miserable, not having slept a wink last night. Rafe's desertion hurt her self-esteem, she admitted honestly. Today she promised herself not to let a single emotion show. Today she'd show Rafe that she was a businesswoman first, interested in him solely as a neighbor. Today she'd forget all about their embrace or die trying.

Andy was over at a friend's house for the rest of the day. Cass needed to get as far away from Rafe as possible. She wanted to finish her business in the neighborhood and leave. The thought of spending the entire day at home, with him directly across the street, made her soul ache.

The door creaked open, and a rush of cool air beckoned her inside. The smell of new wood and freshly laid carpet teased at her senses. Curious about the interior, Cass glanced over Rafe's naked shoulder into the dark, cavernous rooms.

His silver eyes were red-rimmed this morning, and the rough stubble on his neck and face should have made him look tough and scary, but instead he seemed vulnerable. As much as she wanted to believe Rafe would never allow himself to be weak, she recognized the exposed nerves for what they were.

He stood stock-still, his gaze sweeping over her. The force of his will seemed to touch her, and she couldn't look away. Running a hand through his dark, curly hair, he motioned her inside.

Cass wanted to keep their meeting impersonal, and she couldn't do that on his turf. She declined his invitation by shaking her head. Wiping her sweaty palms on her linen skirt, Cass took a deep breath and gathered her thoughts.

"Cass, I was—"

"Mr. Santini," she interrupted smoothly, and paused for a moment to make sure she had his attention. "I'm here on behalf of the association. I've had several complaints about the lawn ornaments, and the grass has got to be mowed."

He reached out to touch her, and Cass flinched away from him without meaning to. His eyes narrowed, and he stepped forward. Cass refused to back away from him, knowing that once she started to retreat she'd never regain the lost ground.

"Okay, I'll mow it today," he said, coming out onto the porch and leaning against the railing. "Cass, I want to—"

"Mr. Santini, you have three days to mow your lawn or you will be fined," Cass said over his words. She didn't want to think about last night, much less talk about it. Rafe was so stubborn. Why couldn't he ignore the embrace as she was planning to do?

Dammit! Even with his eyes red rimmed and his face showing the lack of a good night's sleep he looked wonderful to her. Why did he have to look so good this morning? Especially since she felt frumpy and tired after her sleepless night. He should have been plagued with the same restlessness or look half as bad as she did.

As usual he wore low-slung jeans and his chest was bare. She planned to search the Owner's Agreement and find a ruling against walking around without a shirt on. She couldn't think, when faced with that naked torso. His washboard stomach and rippling muscles were extremely distracting.

"I said I'd mow it today," he snapped, sounding a bit angry. She couldn't blame him. Her mind felt like an overloaded computer chip forced to take on an abundance of memory. Cass knew it was time to leave before she lost control of her emotions and pride and demanded to know why he'd walked away from her last night.

"Yes, you did. Goodbye, Mr. Santini. Don't forget to remove those lawn decorations."

"Cassandra Gambrel, stop right there." The icy tone in his voice convinced her he meant business. She stopped and glanced over her shoulder at him.

"Did you have a Home Owner's Agreement question?" she asked, praying he did. Because if he tried to mention that out-of-this-world kiss one more time she'd lose it.

"You know damn well I don't."

Always swearing, this man, she thought, latching on to something she could use to turn the conversation. "Rafe— Mr. Santini, I'd appreciate it if you wouldn't cuss."

"I'd appreciate it if you wouldn't be obtuse," he said, glaring at her with such intensity Cass feared he'd developed X-ray vision and would burn her skin off.

"I'm not," she said in reply, unable to think of a decent comeback.

Rafe lunged down the steps and Cass held up her hand. "Stop right there you...you...hot-tempered...Italian." She spun on her heel, intent on leaving that overgrown Neanderthal in the dust, but Rafe burst out laughing.

"What do you think is so funny?"

"Cass, the look on your face," he said between loud chuckles. "Absolutely priceless."

She allowed herself a small grin, realizing how ridiculous she'd sounded. Was she destined to make a fool of herself every time she was near this man? Sometimes she took life too seriously. Especially when she was tired and unsure. "Sorry."

She wanted to leave, but he stopped her, this time with a light touch on her elbow. She longed to be stronger, to pull away and leave, but from the moment he'd opened the door, she'd wanted to touch him. To feel him touching her.

"Raphael Santini, let me go."

"I can't," he said so softly she had trouble hearing him.

Cass's heart sank as Rafe led her to the front porch and tugged her down to sit beside him on the step. He put his arm around her shoulders and caught her chin in his firm grasp. "Okay, lady. Not a word until I'm finished. Agreed?"

She nodded, afraid to trust her voice. A strange quivering began in her stomach and spread throughout her body. Rafe had never looked so serious before.

"First, I want to apologize for my abrupt departure last night."

She opened her mouth, and Rafe placed his palm gently but firmly over her lips. "Not a word. I left you because my control was gone and if I'd stayed…"

Cass's heart accelerated as the meaning behind his words sank in. Had he left because he hadn't trusted himself to stay? "Are you saying this to make me feel better about what happened? I know I'm not the type of woman to drive men wild with desire."

"I don't know about other men, but you make me crazy with just a glimpse of those long legs…or the way your face softens when you watch Andy play. Lady, everything about you turns me on."

"Then why did you leave?" she asked, before covering her face with her hands. She couldn't believe she'd had the nerve to ask him that. But she needed to understand. Something was happening between them, something new and unsure. Cass felt alive for the first time since Carl's death.

He gently tugged her hands away from her face. "Because you aren't the type of woman who sleeps with a man just for the pleasure of it. I know that and so do you." He paused, visibly searching for the right words. "Cass, you need someone who can offer you a home and family. I'm not that type of man."

She understood that Rafe was afraid she'd be measuring him for a tuxedo and a wedding ring if he showed her the least bit of attention. Cass couldn't fault his reasoning. She would like to find a husband for herself and a father for Andy. "I don't know you," she said simply, hoping he'd understand.

"I know, and that's why I left." He sighed—a deep lonely sound. "I have no idea where we should go from here. Or even if we should try."

Cass reached up to take his hand in hers. The skin of his callused palm soothed away her fears. This man had a deep well of caring hidden inside, and part of her would always wonder what might have been if she didn't give this all that she had. "Want to try to be friends?"

"I want a hell of a lot more than that." His gaze met hers, and she could see the blaze of passion still burning there. "I spent the whole night pacing the floor and didn't come up with one workable option, lady. But I want you like I've never wanted a woman before."

His words sent sparks dancing throughout her body. Cass was honest enough to admit that she wanted Rafe, too, more than even he could imagine. No other man had ever aroused her senses the way he did. "I want you, too."

He leaned down, brushing his lips against her forehead in a caress so sweet she wanted to cry. "Then we'll take it slowly and get to know each other."

Later that afternoon Rafe moved restlessly in the hard-backed chair. Hundreds of people swarmed around under the large, striped tent. Everyone searching for the perfect antique to fill their home. Cass had left him guarding their seats while she examined the offerings of today's estate sale.

A rush of floral perfume alerted him to Cass's presence before she perched delicately on the edge of her chair. "I found the perfect piece. You are going to love it."

Excitement made her ginger-colored eyes sparkle with the life and vitality he'd come to expect from her. She bit the side of her lip to keep from revealing her smile, a perfect row of white teeth against the peachy-pink color of her lips. He remembered the texture and taste of her mouth and longed to sample it again. "What did you find?"

"A bed," she said in a rush.

At first he thought she had to be kidding. It was the one piece of furniture that carried more connotations than even he could come up with. He raised one eyebrow and winked at her. "A bed?"

"It's an eighteenth-century bed. The carvings on the headboard and footboard match the railing in my house. This is so exciting. I thought I'd never find another carved piece as exquisite as the stair rail."

And Rafe knew in that moment that he'd never find another woman as special as Cass Gambrel. She found joy in things that others didn't.

"I wish I could keep it," she said.

"Why can't you?"

"I don't have the room for it. But it's exquisite. You should go look at it. Lot 629."

Rafe doubted that he'd buy the bed, but something in Cass's eyes convinced him to go and look at it. "Come with me. I won't know a good buy from a piece of junk."

She hesitated, clearly worried whether she should go with him or not. "Okay. It's over here."

He trailed behind Cass as she led the way through the large two-story house. Inside, the rooms were steamy, but the heat didn't bother him. It was nothing compared to the fire she set off inside him. He followed her trimly clad figure as she went unerringly to the stairs and climbed to the upper level.

She paused at an open doorway and motioned for him to go inside. His gaze skipped over the four-poster bed at first, but then went immediately back to it.

Rafe circled the velvet enshrouded bed. The footboard and headboard *were* hand carved. Rafe caressed the intricate design, admiring the hours of work that must have gone into creating it.

The heavy velvet canopy and curtains had faded with time, but the material hadn't rotted. He pulled the curtain aside and whistled softly under his breath.

A sheer curtain of white silk veiled the bed in mystery. Cass pushed the fabric aside, "Look at the inner headboard design."

He tested the softness of the mattress with his palm. It sank beneath his hand, softer than a cloud. The bed stood high above the ground.

"This bed was made for lovemaking," he said, his voice almost reverent. His mind filled with images of Cass lying on its downy softness, waiting for him.

He imagined the feel of satin sheets against his back, their coolness in contrast with the heat of her skin. He felt the tickling length of her sable-colored hair as it brushed against his chest. The soft heat of her mouth as he ravaged it with his own lips.

He pictured the white, filmy curtain enshrouding them like a warm, comforting fog, keeping the world out. The bed would be their only link to reality. The two of them on a physical journey to unite their bodies. He sighed, imagining the perfection of that joining.

Rafe pictured Cass lying on her back, beckoning him closer. He wouldn't deny her—couldn't. He lowered his body on top of hers, reveling in her curves and hollows— her body fitting his with such heartbreaking accuracy.

Her voice teasingly calling to him...

"Rafe?"

Reality broke through, and he turned to her. The tension in his loins made the movement uncomfortable. Hell, he thought, he had to make love to her soon. There was no question in his mind. Never had fantasy seemed so real.

"I'll buy it," he said. "You can refinish it for me."

"Rafe, this bed is going to go for top dollar today. It's a real antique. Do you have any idea what it costs?"

Hell, no, but then he hadn't had any sane ideas since last night when he'd realized that a single mom was turning him inside out. "I want that bed, Cass."

"Why? You don't own any other antiques."

"Because all I can picture in my head is the two of us on that bed. This filmy curtain keeping the world out while I love you out of your mind."

She flushed and glanced down. "Oh."

"Yes, 'oh.' Now will you help me buy the bed and refinish it?"

She nodded. Ignoring the thrill that shot through her at the idea of her and Rafe in that bed, she said, "It really is the most beautiful thing I've ever seen."

No, the bed wasn't, Rafe thought. Cass was. Every little thing about her made him realize how much he needed her, how much she'd affected him in the short time he'd known her. "Ah, hell."

"Rafe, really. No more cussing."

He smiled to himself as he followed her out of the room. The day he quit cussing he'd know he was a goner. Hell, he hoped that day never came.

# Five

A persistent buzzing interrupted Cass's blatantly erotic dream. She ignored the sound, concentrating instead on the feelings swamping her body. Her blood pounded as she kissed her way down Rafe's torso. The springy hair on his chest tickled her nose, and she paused to rub her cheek against him. Rafe's hands were suddenly in her hair, pulling her up his body.

He nibbled on her neck, then his lips moved lower and lower…no, wait, that buzz was coming from outside. What the heck was going on outside her window?

Her body felt flushed and achy, and she knew that she would never be as brave in person as she'd been in her fantasy. She'd seduced Rafe Santini. And she wasn't finished. She wanted to go back to sleep and get to the good stuff.

How she wished she had the courage to do it in real life. But there was something awesome and scary about his unconcealed sensuality. It made her feel flustered and strangely excited. She couldn't handle a repeat of the other night when he'd kissed her and left. The loud noise again invaded her thoughts. She glanced at the clock and groaned out loud.

"Six o'clock in the morning," she muttered, rubbing her face in the pillow and hoping the noise would go away. Cass wasn't a woman to stay in bed until noon, but she never rose with the sun, especially on Saturday. It was the one day a week she could sleep in without guilt.

Irrationally, the sound seemed louder now that she was awake. Cass grabbed her robe and walked to the window, searching the street for the culprit. Most of her neighbors worked nine-to-five during the week and slept in late on the weekends. There was even a mandate in the Owner's Agreement that stated no loud noises before seven o'clock in the morning.

It came as no great surprise to see Rafe Santini pushing a mower. He was mowing her lawn. He had on his skimpy nylon running shorts and headphones. As usual his tanned chest was bare, and Cass licked her lips remembering the feel of those muscled arms around her.

What was that crazy man doing? He glanced up at her bedroom window and waved when he saw her standing there. Cass wiggled her fingers back at him as a warm, fuzzy feeling enveloped her. She leaned against the cool glass and wondered how she was going to handle the situation.

Once again she was going to have to issue a warning to Mr. Santini. Deep down she knew that Rafe was out there for only one reason. He was a kind, caring man beneath that wild-boy facade. Last night she'd mentioned that she hated yard work.

Rafe was in conflict with the Owner's Agreement, but she couldn't tell him that. She sighed. How could she chastise him for being wonderful? No one had ever gone out of their way for her before. She'd been doing chores she hated since...well as long as she could remember.

She wondered if it was becoming a game to him. Last week he'd watered his lawn during the day, which was not only in breech of his Owner's Agreement but also against the law. She'd seen a police officer leaving a ticket on his front door.

Rafe brought out new feelings in her that were strange and scary. Cass knew that she couldn't fine Rafe, but she had to quiet him before he woke others in the neighborhood and they complained.

Cass dressed quickly in a pair of faded jeans and her Orlando Magic T-shirt. She ignored the reasons why she chose to wear that particular shirt today. She pulled her hair into a ponytail and shoved her feet into canvas boat shoes on her way down the stairs.

"Rafe," she yelled from the sidewalk. He continued mowing, not even glancing her way when he turned in her direction.

She stepped carefully onto the grass and stood directly in Rafe's path. He turned off the mower, and silence fell around her like a warm blanket on a chilly morning. He removed his headphones and sunglasses. God, he was so sexy. What did he see in her?

"Good morning, Cass."

His husky, morning voice soothed her jumbled thoughts and feelings. She suddenly forgot why she'd come outside and at the same time regretted that she hadn't been there sooner. That tone made her want to curl up against his chest and never leave him.

"Miss me?" he asked, staring at her mouth.

She nodded. Was he thinking about kissing her? She hoped so. Then Cass remembered the reason they were both standing in the middle of her backyard. "You can't mow this early in the morning."

"What?" he asked, still looking at her lips.

He ran his hand across his bare chest, and Cass's gaze followed the movement. "You're in violation of the Owner's Agreement again."

"What'd I do this time? Hell, I was just being neighborly and saving you from paying a fine."

The aggrieved tone made Cass doubt his knowledge of the all-quiet mandate. Rafe was a very busy man. This last week he'd been gone from dawn to dusk. She knew he hadn't had time to read the contract. She'd seen him out running only once, and even then he'd seemed overly tired.

"I know," she said, stepping closer to him. He seemed so out of sorts. She brushed her finger against his jaw. "I hated to come down here, but I had to, before you woke any of the neighbors."

"Why?" he asked, his silver gaze so intense she couldn't look away.

"Why what?" A foot of space separated them, and Cass thought about closing the gap. She could feel the heat from him where she stood, and smell the sweat he'd worked up.

"Why did you 'hate to come down here'?" He teased her by reaching for her but only to brush the bangs out of her eyes.

Honesty demanded that she tell him the truth, but leaving herself that vulnerable was hard. She decided to phrase her reasons in a way that would distract him. "I just thought it was sweet of you."

"Sweet? No way, lady. I'm not sweet. I just can't handle the distraction of you in your mowing shorts."

Cass smiled at his words. He stepped closer to her. Now only an inch of space separated him. Cass's fingers tingled with the need to touch his sweat-slicked skin. "What distraction? Those shorts are baggy."

"They're faded and they cling to your backside." He winked at her as he made that outrageous remark.

"Rafe!"

"You asked. By the way, you've got nice buns, too, honey."

Cass gasped. "Santini, shut up."

He laughed out loud, the sound booming in the early

morning silence. "Tell me about the rule I broke this time."

Cass struggled to forget his comment about her body. "You can't run any power equipment before seven o'clock."

"How much is it going to cost me this time?" he asked, but there was little heat in his words.

"The fine is two hundred dollars, but I'm only issuing you a warning."

He tilted his head to the side as he considered her answer. "Doesn't that go against the rules?"

"Technically, yes. But I haven't had any calls about the noise."

He stepped closer, placing his hands on her shoulders. "Is there really a law against noise?"

"Yes." She moistened her suddenly dry lips. She longed to feel his mouth on hers. What was happening to her? "When are you going to read that agreement?"

"I skimmed it." His breath brushed across her cheek.

"Not closely enough, if you didn't notice the fine." Her voice sounded husky, and she knew that if he didn't kiss her soon, she was going to take matters into her own hands. Her breasts brushed against his naked chest. Rafe felt so good next to her.

He pulled her more firmly into contact with his body. "I had other things on my mind."

Cass lowered her eyes, his mouth was hard, a strong mouth that promised integrity with each word he spoke. "What things?"

Her voice barely sounded above a whisper. Rafe lowered his head, resting his cheek against hers. He rubbed his stubble-covered jaw against hers.

He smelled wonderfully masculine. She wanted to feel him wrapped around her as they'd been on the ladder the other day. She moved back a small space, wanting to see his expression. She raised her eyes to his face and saw a spark of teasing there, but it was dominated by the fire of passion.

"Ms. Gambrel, you are the most distracting woman," he said, and finally kissed her. His lips touching hers were light and caressing, not fierce and demanding.

Cass gave in to the temptation and wrapped her arms around Rafe's sweat-slicked shoulders. He felt so good, so solid in her embrace that she unconsciously tightened her arms.

The kiss was the promise of a new day. Everything that Cass wanted from Rafe seemed to be there in his arms, his touch, his taste. She curled her fingers into his thick hair and luxuriated in the feel of him, never wanting to let go.

"Where's Andy?" Rafe asked after long minutes had passed.

"Sleeping. I planned to invite you to breakfast," she said, dropping a teasing kiss on his lips. She ran her forefinger along the edge of his neck and down the center of his chest. "But only if you wear some decent shorts."

"I thought you liked my buns."

"What's with you this morning?" Cass felt the heat of her blush and rested her forehead against his shoulder. "If you had any finesse you'd never mention buns again—yours or mine."

He used his thumb to lift her chin. His eyes were gentler than she'd seen them before, and Cass felt a spark of caring unfold and begin to turn to...affection. She backed away from him, both physically and emotionally.

"I better get back inside the house. I'll be serving breakfast in an hour."

"I'll be there. Thanks for the warning, Cass." He pushed the now silent lawn mower across the street.

"Don't forget to dress decently."

He laughed out loud—a deep, booming sound that made her smile. She shook her head and hurried inside to fix breakfast, pretending that she wasn't excited about having her sexy neighbor to breakfast.

* * *

Cass was humming softly when Rafe walked into her workshop later that morning. He'd promised her to keep Andy busy and outside so that she could start refinishing the bed he'd purchased at the auction. But he didn't mind— the little kid was growing on him.

Rafe liked the way the boy asked intelligent questions. Andy knew when to talk and when to be quiet. A lesson Rafe hadn't learned while his dad was alive. Rafe cautioned himself not to care, but sometimes it was easy to forget his own warning.

Cass kneeled at the top of the bed, cleaning the headboard. She was absorbed in her work, and Rafe thought she'd never looked lovelier. He paused at the door, loath to disturb her.

Here was Cassandra the woman. This was her calling, what she loved to do, and it showed in each movement of her hands. She carefully cleaned the detailed carving, touching it with firm, competent strokes.

A sudden image of those same fingers on his body made Rafe want to groan out loud. Lord, he wanted her with a desire that was beginning to feel like obsession.

He should leave. Walk away before things got any more complicated. But dammit, never had a woman touched him on so many levels. This woman and her son were becoming important, and he cursed his own stupidity for allowing that to happen.

Her long legs were curled beneath her in a position that he knew he couldn't have held for thirty seconds. He loved her legs. They were slender, yet firm, and he wanted to feel them wrapped around his waist. Every time he saw her, sex got in the way.

He cleared his throat. "Ready for a break?"

"I don't need a break," she said with a teasing grin. "I've been...how did you put it the other day? Lazing around in the shade while you worked diligently in the sun."

He laughed as he stepped closer to her. He'd forgotten how good it was to share laughter and smiles with someone. Bowing deeply, he said, "I humbly apologize for my lack of appreciation for the time and effort required by your occupation."

Cass gasped out loud. Then jumped from the bed, hurrying across the room to him. She put her hand on his forehead and peered deeply into his eyes. "Rafe? Are you sick? Do you have a fever? Or did an alien take over your body?"

"Watch it, Gambrel. I don't have to put up with this nonsense from you," he said, pulling her closer for a kiss. Her lips always tempted him. At night when he lay in bed all he could think of was her mouth. He would remember her sweet smile, and desire would flare out of control. Damn, he wanted her.

"I'm serious, Santini. This is the first time I've heard you apologize. I didn't think you had it in you."

He rolled his eyes and released her neck, tugging on her ponytail the way he'd done to his sister many years ago. Angelica's sweet face danced through his mind's eye before he could stop it. "How's the bed coming?"

"Good. Why?" she asked.

"Want to go to the movies?" he blurted out, feeling awkward. Where was the cool sophistication he'd cultivated so many years ago? Where was the suave gentleman that had once attended the theater and opera with elegant women?

Rafe had turned his back on more than just memories. He'd forgotten how to be a gentleman, and he wasn't sure that was all bad, because it had protected some inner part of his soul. But Cass was stirring up old memories and remembered guilt.

"Now?" she asked, bringing him back to attention.

"Yeah, there's a baseball movie I thought Andy might like to see." Great, Santini, make her think you just want to take the kid out. In truth, Rafe wanted to sit in a dark theater with her by his side, sharing popcorn and soft whispers.

"Okay," she said simply. "I'd like to go. But I have to warn you that Andy likes to sit in the front of the theater and eats about twenty dollars worth of candy. Just watching him is enough to give me a bellyache."

"You allow that?" Rafe found it hard to believe that Cass, who served bran muffins and buckwheat pancakes for breakfast, would permit her son to eat junk food.

She gave him a sharp look. He knew from past experience that Cass didn't like to have her parenting techniques questioned. "We don't go to the movies that often, so I don't see the harm in indulging his sweet tooth on occasion."

"I wasn't criticizing," he said, honestly meaning it. Cass did a better job raising Andy than most couples did with their children.

"Yes, you were. I understand how easy it is to stand on the outside and make snap judgments that appear sound. Don't think that I find this decision an easy one, it isn't. But Andy's father used to take him to the movies on Saturday afternoons, and they'd eat junk food until their stomachs ached."

Rafe understood what he hadn't before. He forgot that Cass had to be both father and mother to her son. That sometimes she had to fill a place in her son's life that she felt insecure about. "I'm sorry, Cass. I was out of line."

She was silent for so long, he wondered if he'd damaged any chance they had to be friends. And that hurt. As much as he wanted Cass in his bed, he needed her friendship.

"You weren't out of line. I overreacted. I hate that he eats all that junk food. But you should have seen his face the first time I took him to see a show after Carl died. It was hard, to go against my own instincts and buy candy for him."

"Come here, baby." Rafe hugged Cass to his chest. He'd never really considered the difficulties of parenthood.

Never having been a father, he hadn't worried about the problem much. But Cass obviously needed someone to be supportive of her decisions and to help her with the difficult ones. What was he doing in her life?

Bone-deep instinct told him that she must care for him. Cass would never allow herself to start a relationship with a man that was fleeting and inconsequential to either of them.

Cass rubbed her face against his chest, and Rafe was suddenly glad that he seldom wore a shirt. He liked the feeling of her smooth skin against his. He held her until she pulled away.

In her eyes he could read gratitude and some other less easily defined emotion. Run, his instincts said. Get far away from this lady before it's too late. But instead he brushed a light kiss on the top of her head.

"I'll pick you up in twenty minutes. Andy and I already checked out the time."

"What if I'd said no?" she asked.

"You didn't," he replied, walking to the door. "Go get changed, you only have twenty minutes, and Andy assures me that you will be hard-pressed to be ready on time."

Cass groaned out loud and Rafe smiled as he left. Anticipation followed him home, and for once he didn't temper it. Damn, but it felt good to be alive.

The night air was cooler than it had been since last winter, and Cass shivered a bit in her short-sleeved blouse. She was tempted to go inside and get a sweater, but Rafe moved closer, draping his arm around her shoulder. His body heat surrounded her, taking the chill from her and replacing it with his warmth.

"Better?" he asked, softly.

She nodded, not wanting to speak. The evening was alive with noise. Chirping crickets, the call of the whippoorwill and the distant sound of traffic all blended together to create a symphony.

Andy had gone to bed shortly after nine. Cass and Rafe had adjourned to the porch with a bottle of wine. She planned to invite him to join her family for Thanksgiving, but didn't know how to ask him. He seemed alone here in Florida and she wondered if he had family elsewhere. He never talked about his past. She'd never known an Italian who didn't have family and lots of it.

She shivered again and Rafe pulled her closer. "Want to go inside, Cassie?"

"No," she murmured. She liked the way he called her Cassie. No one ever had. She was too independent and stubborn to be anything other than Cass to her family and friends. "Thanksgiving is next week."

"Umm-hmm," he said, rubbing his face against her hair.

"Do you have plans?" Cass reached for his hand, weaving their fingers together. She liked the contrast in their skin colors, his deeply tanned, hers a paler shade.

"No. I like to spend the holidays alone."

"What about your family?" she asked. She sensed an underlying loneliness when he spoke of the holidays. There was so much she didn't know about Rafe. So many layers to this man that she hadn't explored. So many reasons not to get involved with him. But those same reasons also drew her to him, made her want to know him better.

Instead of answering, he kissed her neck. Cass shivered again, but the nature of the gesture had changed. Sensual delight coursed through her this time.

She wanted to protest and force him to answer her questions. But the isolation she sensed in him convinced her to allow him what he needed. She tilted her head to the side to give Rafe more access to the place on her neck.

He freed his hand from hers, rubbing her back before he hugged her closer to him. She wished that he'd feel as confident with her emotionally as he did physically. She loved feeling his strong, hard chest against hers. She resented the fact that he wore a shirt.

She felt his hand at her breast through the thin material

of her silk blouse and ached to feel his palm against her skin without the barrier. She moaned when his mouth met hers. The kiss was so much more than the earlier embrace had been.

This meeting of their mouths was a prelude to lovemaking, and Cass didn't delude herself that it was anything else. But she wasn't ready for that final act of commitment. She could still pretend she didn't love him if they didn't sleep together.

She pulled back. Rafe's gaze met hers. "I know," he said softly. "I'll go home."

Cass wanted to ask him to stay but knew she didn't have the right. He started down the porch steps. "Good night, Rafe."

"Night, Cassie." He strode back to her, kissing her lingeringly on the lips.

"I don't want you to leave." Her voice was husky with passion, but squeaky with embarrassment, and sounded odd to her. She blushed at the tone and hid her face against his chest.

"You don't want me to stay, either," he said. And Cass knew he was right. As much as she liked him she wasn't ready for anything other than friendship and caring. Oh, Rafe, she thought. What are we going to do when this passion spins out of control? And she knew that it would before long.

# Six

Rafe held a cup of coffee in his right hand as he stepped out onto the porch. If he was outside before seven-thirty, he could watch Cass leaving to take Andy to school. She always looked bright and cheerful. His day seemed to go smoother if he saw her first thing.

He glanced across the street noticing the empty driveway. Ah, hell, he thought, as a feeling strangely like disappointment swamped him. He hated to admit it, but he was beginning to depend on Cass Gambrel. Even more daunting was the knowledge that he cared about her.

Last night he'd felt something change inside. Bottled emotions had sprung free of the containment he'd put them in. Cass thought he'd placed her desires in front of his own. Truth to tell, when he'd kissed her, the rush of emotion he'd felt scared him.

Even his desire for Anne, whom he'd wanted so badly he'd ignored his responsibility to his family, hadn't been this sharp. Ah, hell, Cass was dangerous to him, but his lack of control could be lethal to her.

His self-control was tenuous at best around her. Never before had the wanting been so sharp. He found himself thinking of her at the most inconvenient times. Yesterday he'd almost walked through a skylight on the construction site. The crew had teased him endlessly about his near mishap. This had to stop, but he wasn't sure how to end his torment without hurting Cass. Simple seduction wasn't going to work. She needed more than that, and when Rafe was with her, so did he.

After years of isolation and short meaningless encounters, the one woman he shouldn't be interested in was the only one who made him feel alive. She forced him to take stock of his life. He saw the emptiness that had always been there, only now it bothered him. Dammit, she stirred up old memories and feelings he'd thought were safely buried.

He turned to go back inside to get ready for work when a brown, wrapped package caught his eye. Propped against the wall next to the door frame, the innocuous box drew him like a nail to a magnet. "What the hell," he muttered.

Tundra bounded up the stairs sniffing and drooling on the package. "What do you think, girl?"

The dog barked in a friendly way that told Rafe the scent was familiar to the husky. Setting his coffee on the railing, he stooped to retrieve the package. He loosened the twine on the box, knowing instinctively that the package was from Cass.

A note fluttered to the ground. The floral perfume he associated with Cass drifted from the letter. Intrigued, he crouched down to retrieve the pastel-colored paper.

He fingered the fragile stuff for a moment. The light color looked ridiculous in his work-roughened hands. Sometimes he forgot the traces left by his trade, forgot he couldn't ever be a gentleman again because he'd chosen a different path long ago.

The handwriting was graceful and feminine, but also

strong, much like Cass herself. He pictured her writing the note in her bedroom, wearing that frilly robe she'd had on when they'd first met. He studied the script before reading the letter:

"I believe a gentleman should be properly attired at all times. Happy Thanksgiving."

Rafe chuckled over the note. Tundra grabbed the twine and dashed off the porch. He watched the dog go before looking down at the brown wrapping. Seven shirts in varying colors and fabrics were enclosed. He grabbed a khaki-colored cotton T-shirt and headed into the house to take a shower. A gift of this type demanded that he reciprocate. But how?

Some type of clothing, he decided. A one-of-a-kind nightgown. He knew just the place to order it from. Cass liked to have pretty things in her house, but he noticed her own clothing was serviceable. It was something she wouldn't buy for herself.

He sensed that Cass had meant the shirts in both a humorous and a serious way. His half-naked state bothered her more than he'd realized. Of course, he wasn't going to run around fully clothed in the heat of summer, but truth to tell the fall weather had turned cool enough for a shirt not to be a bother.

Fifteen minutes later Rafe walked out to his Jaguar and was sitting in the car when Cass pulled into her driveway. He pulled across the street and rolled down the window.

Her sunglasses covered the majority of her face, but a pretty blush covered the rest. "Morning, Cassie."

Her eyes dropped to his chest, and a brief smile graced her face. Her sable-colored hair was tied at the back of her neck, making her look younger than she was.

"Mr. Santini," she said. Her voice was soft and gentle, but held a teasing note. "Nice shirt."

"Thanks," he said, grinning up at her. "I've been told that a gentleman should always be properly attired."

Her blush intensified, and Rafe felt his grin widen. She

smiled in return, and his stomach tightened with emotion. Rafe knew the time for waiting was over. He wanted to spend the evening with her on a real date.

"Rafe, I wanted to invite you to have dinner with us on Thursday."

He stared at her for a long moment before shaking his head. He wanted to have dinner with Cass—hell, he'd been about to invite her out—but not on a holiday. Holidays reminded him of all he'd lost. He had plans for Thanksgiving, and they didn't include being surrounded by happy, loving people.

"It's Thanksgiving, Rafe, and I thought you'd like to meet my family. I always host that holiday. We go to my mother's on Christmas."

She was rambling, and Rafe knew that he'd hurt her feelings by declining her offer. "I can't, Cass. I'm sorry."

"That's okay," she said, but the hurt lingered in her eyes. "You have plans?"

"Yeah." He couldn't tell her that he planned to go to Jimmy's, a downtown sports bar and get drunk. That only after he'd had a bottle of Scotch could he forestall the memories of his parents' death.

"With family?"

Her innocent little questions were making it harder for him to answer her. "I've got to go."

He rolled up the window and gunned the engine. He had to get away from Cass. He had to get away from his home and the memories that were crowding in on him. He had to forget that his mother would have loved Cass and that his father would have doted on Andy. That the Gambrels would have been welcomed lovingly into the Santini clan. Except that there wasn't a Santini clan anymore. Only one lone survivor.

Rafe cursed under his breath until Cass's image couldn't be seen in the mirror. He sped the entire way to the construction site, hoping that mindless work would take his mind off of Cass. But he knew that it wouldn't.

* * *

Two days later Cass sat on the floor next to the antique bed Rafe had purchased, trying not to think about him. The bed was almost finished, and she'd be glad when the job was complete. The bed made her think of Rafe, and her thoughts weren't always proper. In fact some had been downright erotic.

It was the man's own fault. Every evening he ran through the neighborhood in those indecent shorts of his, making her remember what he'd felt like when he'd kissed her. She'd had another dream about Rafe and his bed last night. Her subconscious had yet to realize that he was ignoring her, that he'd given up on his seduction of her.

She tightened her fingers around the bedpost. This piece of furniture was one of her best efforts. She ran her hand lovingly over the carved footboard and forced away the image of Rafe lounging there in nothing but his running shorts.

It was harder than it should be, she thought, not to think of him. The man had gotten to her, and he didn't even know it. The doorbell rang, interrupting her thoughts. She hurried through her house to the front door as the bell sounded again.

"Who's there?" she asked. Cass glanced through the peephole and saw a man from a well-known delivery service.

"UPS delivery for Mrs. Gambrel."

Cass opened the door, trying to remember if she'd ordered anything lately. She signed for the package before going back inside the house. She opened the box and was surprised to see a red satin nightgown.

"Holy cow," she said. The only person who could have sent this was Rafe. Only a man intent on seduction would buy this negligee. Only Rafe would have the nerve to send her an item this blatant and then proceed to ignore her.

She pulled the gown from the box and blushed when she noticed that the front of the gown was made of sheer red

lace. The deep red satin dipped in a vee at the back almost
to the waist. This gown wasn't made for sleeping, but for
tempting. She would never have the nerve to wear something like this.

Why had he sent it? She remembered the morning she'd
given him the shirts. When he'd first come over to her yard,
he'd looked tender, kind, as if he'd found something he'd
lost.

But then he'd turned away from her, becoming the cold,
unemotional neighbor that he'd been in the beginning. Rafe
had changed in those moments, and she knew why. He was
afraid she was sizing him up for a wedding ring. She
couldn't blame him; she was a single mother and someday
she'd like to remarry. But she knew Rafe wasn't in the
market for a ready-made family.

She shook the gown searching for a card, and one tum-
bled to the ground. She half hoped that he'd sent the nightgown after their confrontation, but logically knew that he
must've sent it earlier. Wary, but excited, she slid the card
from the envelope, slowly building the anticipation in her
mind. It said:

"I believe a lady should be properly attired at night."

Had her words sounded that arrogant? She glanced at the
beautiful gown and fought against tears. No man had ever
given her such a gift, not even Carl. From him she'd gotten
food mixers and vacuum cleaners.

The sudden barking of a dog drew her to the window.
Rafe and Tundra came into view, and she couldn't help
wondering if he hadn't planned his arrival that way, though
she doubted he knew the exact time they'd deliver her
gown.

Suddenly she was angry at herself and Rafe. Here was a
man that she wanted to get to know. A man she wanted to
spend more of her time with. A man that she wanted in her
bed. But they weren't suited to each other.

Her own past experiences and Rafe's worked against
them. Something in Rafe's life had taught him to shy away

from commitment, even a short-term one. And her upbringing made loving him without a commitment an impossibility.

She hurried onto her porch, determined to talk to Rafe. The first thing she needed to do was find out why he'd shied away from her Thanksgiving invitation. She knew him well enough to know his "other plans" were just an excuse. Heck, he didn't have to meet her family if the thought made him uncomfortable.

"Raphael Santini," she said in a loud voice.

"Ma'am," he answered politely.

"I want to talk to you." She walked to the edge of the porch, pausing at the top of the steps. She contemplated climbing down, but wanted to be on equal footing with Rafe.

He crossed the street and climbed the steps. He smelled like he always did—masculine and sweaty. Cass noticed that his gaze dropped to her hands, and she remembered the gown. "Thank you."

"You're welcome. I meant the gift to be something—" He shrugged and glanced away from the gown. "Never mind. The reason no longer exists."

"Tell me anyway," she demanded, feeling braver than she'd ever been before, urged on by the desire to understand why he'd send her this lovely gift if he didn't intend to see her wear it.

"You won't like the reason."

She stared at him, waiting for his response, willing him to answer. She wasn't backing down this time. She needed to understand this man she was beginning to love.

"I knew you wouldn't buy a gown like this for yourself." He reached out to touch the red satin. "And I wanted to think of you sleeping in something as beautiful as you are."

"Rafe," she said, her voice softer than a whisper. She thought she was going to cry. He'd obviously given the gift some thought. She wished now that she'd met him earlier in her life, before events had shaped her into the person she was. She didn't regret Andy and wouldn't change him for anyone, but part of her soul ached at the thought of never experiencing love with Rafe.

"The gown doesn't come close to your loveliness, Cass."

He brushed his finger against her cheek, and she leaned into the caress. They stood like that for long minutes until Cass remembered she had something else to ask him.

"What did I say the other morning to upset you?" she asked. "I've gone over it a hundred times in my head and can't figure out how I offended you."

Rafe muttered a curse word under his breath and pulled her roughly to him. He rubbed her back and dropped a soft kiss on the top of her head. "It isn't anything you said."

"Help me understand."

He sat down on the porch steps and tugged Cass down next to him. "My parents were killed in a car accident on Thanksgiving."

"Oh, Rafe. I'm so sorry." Cass understood the pain that he felt. She knew how the death of a loved one could tear you up inside. But she also knew that Rafe hadn't begun to heal. "Well, you certainly shouldn't spend the day by yourself."

"I plan to go to Jimmy's." His gray eyes were intense, and she stared at him for a few moments before his words sank into her mind.

"Is he a friend of yours?" she asked. She'd never met any of Rafe's crew, perhaps he was spending the day with one of his workers.

"No," he said with a chuckle. "It's an eating establishment."

"I've never heard of it."

"It's downtown, near Church Street Station."

"A bar?"

He nodded soberly and glanced away from her.

"Rafe, alcohol is never the solution," she said sternly.

It was hard to think clearly, though, with his arm draped around her. She forgot all about the lecture she'd been planning to give him. Her pulse rate increased, and she leaned closer to him, offering comfort with her presence.

"I know, Cassie. But it's better than sitting home and remembering."

"Then you should come to my house." She wrapped her hands around one of his. "My brother-in-law is the only man in our family. He'd love the company."

Rafe stared at their joined hands, tightening his fingers briefly. "I think that would be even worse."

Cass stiffened at the insult. "We aren't ogres, Rafe. Tony's nice enough, if you like to talk about football, and I know that you do."

"Calm down, Cass. Your family's probably great—but I don't want to get involved with them. I *won't* allow myself to care, not again."

Cass understood, then, that Rafe was protecting himself from further pain, but also trying to keep from hurting her and Andy. "Thanks for explaining."

He didn't say anything else and neither did she. But Cass felt that new ground had been reached. She wasn't giving up on Rafe. He had the potential to be a wonderful, caring mate and that was her ultimate goal.

The knock at his door had been expected. Rafe knew Cass would try to entice him over to her house. Her nature wouldn't let her ignore him or let him stay at home ignoring her.

But when he opened the door, Andy looked up at him, instead of Cass. The boy was clearly uncomfortable in the dress suit he wore and fidgeted from foot to foot.

"Hi, Andy. What's up?" he asked, leaning against the door frame.

"I'm supposed to tell you that everyone's going to be leaving around six o'clock tonight."

"Okay." Rafe felt something tight inside his chest

loosen up. Leave it to Cass to find a way to let him know he wasn't alone. She had to be the most caring woman he'd ever met.

"Mom said maybe you'd come over for a late supper."

"Thanks for delivering the message, pal."

"That's okay. I couldn't stand it a minute longer. My cousins are all in there."

"What's wrong with your cousins?" Rafe asked. Cass's son intrigued him.

"They're all girls, and they want me to play bride and groom with them. Ugh. I'd rather eat broccoli."

Rafe was careful not to laugh, knowing that Andy would be offended. "I know what you mean, Andy. My sister made me play tea party with her once a week."

"Oh, man. That's awful. Why are girls so gross?"

Well, that was a loaded question, Rafe thought. "They grow out of it, Andy. Trust me."

"You want to come back over there with me? Uncle Tony's locked himself in the den. We could probably sneak in there with him."

Rafe thought he hadn't allowed himself to care, but realized suddenly how much he did. Still, he couldn't resist Andy's forlorn little face. One day couldn't make much difference—the damage had already been done. He'd spend the day, do what he could for the kid and then back off.

"Okay, pal. Wait here while I go change."

Rafe dressed in one of the shirts Cass had given him and clean jeans. He combed his hair and realized his hands were shaking. Families scared him more than anything in the world. What if he did something to endanger poor little Andy? What if he hurt him the way he'd hurt his sister?

He dropped the comb on the bathroom counter. "Straighten up, man."

He put his keys in his pocket and walked out the door, determined to enjoy himself this day. Even if it killed him.

Andy was unusually chatty on the walk across the street. "Uh, Rafe?"

"Yeah, Andy?"

"I wasn't supposed to invite you over or pressure you into anything."

"It's okay—you didn't."

They walked into the kitchen, and Rafe felt as if he'd been thrust back in time. The smells of Thanksgiving surrounded him, the turkey roasting in the oven, pies cooling on the counter, feminine voices all talking at the same time as they bustled around the kitchen preparing hors d'oeuvres.

He expected to see his mother and sister huddled in the mass. It was all so familiar, except they'd had lasagna instead of turkey. Memories overwhelmed him. He couldn't handle it, he thought, then glanced at Cass.

She set her pot holder on the counter and walked to him. When she put her arms around him, he knew he'd be okay. He didn't like the feeling that this one woman held that kind of power over him, but for today it was okay.

"Happy Thanksgiving, Rafe," she said softly, before kissing him on the lips.

Spontaneous applause broke out around the kitchen. Cass blushed and grabbed his hand, dragging him to the center of the room. "Everyone this is…my neighbor from across the street, Rafe Santini. Rafe, this is everyone."

The rest of the day flew by. He chatted with Cass's mother, Iris, who drifted around the kitchen looking graceful and elegant, while smelling distinctly of Chanel. Cass's older sister, Eve, spent twenty minutes telling him about her courtship of Tony. Cass's younger sister, Sara, kept him in stitches while spinning stories about Cass as a child. But the one woman in the room that he couldn't take his eyes off was Cass. She sparkled like a mirror in the sun, catching and reflecting happiness everywhere she went.

Rafe and Tony were recruited into helping mash the potatoes and carve the turkey. Tony was glad for the masculine company and kept Rafe busy talking about football. It was the best Thanksgiving since his parents' death, and he had Cass to thank for it.

# Seven

The need to escape overwhelmed Cass, as the emotion of the day caught up with her that evening. Andy and Rafe sat together on the couch talking quietly about the football game on the television. She put aside her cross-stitch and left the room without saying anything to the men. She'd never thought that Rafe and Andy would be friends.

The cool, crisp evening air beckoned Cass outside. Rafe and Andy were still engrossed in the football game, and Cass didn't have the heart to lecture the two males on the downfalls of professional sports. The mingled sounds of masculine and boyish laughter met her ears and she smiled.

Her quiet son was not the most outgoing of children, but he'd found a way to relate to Rafe Santini. Or maybe it was Rafe who'd found a way to bond with Andy. He was different from the man who'd refused to hold her son's hand at the Magic basketball game. There was a well of caring inside Rafe that he kept contained, but occasionally emotions slipped past his guard.

Her son and Rafe were an unlikely duo. Cass would have wagered the Thanksgiving turkey on Rafe's not showing up at her house today. Somehow Andy had reached out to him in a way she couldn't. Maybe it was a man thing, she thought.

She remembered his gift of the day before. In the soft glow of evening it had been easy to imagine wearing it for Rafe. She'd slept in the gown last night and dreamed once again of him. She didn't understand this hold he had over her inner thoughts.

He had the same power over her son. After their conversation the day before, the last person she'd have expected Rafe to befriend was her son. And perhaps the most vulnerable. Because Andy wouldn't understand when Santini stopped doing things with them.

Rafe had made his position clear to her. He was interested in a short-term, noncommitted relationship. She wanted a long-term commitment. She tried to think of a workable solution, but in her heart she knew there wasn't one.

Her soul ached at the thought of never sleeping with Rafe's arms wrapped around her, of never experiencing the freshness of a new day with him by her side, of never feeling his breath against her cheek first thing in the morning, of never making love with him.

"What's the matter with you," she asked herself quietly. But she knew the answer. Rafe. She sighed, the sound quite pitiful. She didn't like the pathetic path her thoughts were on. She was a strong woman. She always worked her way past obstacles, and this would be no different.

"Cass?"

Rafe's voice startled her. A low, husky sound that brought to mind long nights and slow loving. She imagined that his voice would drop even lower if he saw her in that sexy red gown he'd given her. Heavens, she was turning into a sex fiend.

"Cassie?" he asked again. "Everything okay?"

"Fine, I'm just enjoying the night air." And making myself crazy.

The screen door squeaked as Rafe opened it. The sound was loud and jarring in the quiet night. He stood next to her for a long time not saying a word. The musky scent of his cologne, combined with the smell of the night-blooming jasmine, created a seductive atmosphere.

Cass longed to reach for him, wrap her arms around this strong man and offer him whatever comfort she could. Instead she moved away from him, knowing that if she stayed close, she'd give in to temptation. She sat on the porch swing and tried not to stare at him.

Rafe had both hands braced on the railing and his head bowed. Cass stood up again and went to him. She couldn't leave Rafe by himself...isolated. Not today, of all days.

She knew what he must be feeling. She hated the anniversary of Carl's death. She was an absolute bear to be around on that day. Her family stood by her side, no matter how sullen or moody she was. They comforted and supported her, serving as a buffer between her and the pain, and she wanted to do the same for Rafe. She couldn't let him suffer alone.

Rafe didn't have a large, loving family waiting to help shoulder the load. She wanted to reach out to him and show him that she understood the pain that still felt like a living thing. She longed to cuddle him in her arms and soothe that pain away. But he'd never accept that from her or even admit that he needed solace.

"Is Andy okay?" she asked to distract herself.

"He's sleeping." Rafe put his hands on her shoulder and turned her to face him. "Cass, I want to talk to you."

She nodded, afraid it sounded like goodbye. Maybe being reminded of all he'd lost had reinforced the reasons why he didn't want to be involved with her.

She'd known this was coming. Her family had been too much for him. She couldn't really blame him. Her mother and sisters had been asking leading questions all afternoon. They made Andy's inquisition look like child's play.

In an effort to forestall him, she said, "I'm sorry my mother asked about your parents. I told her to leave it alone. But she feels it's better to talk about problems. I used to always—"

He stopped the rush of words with a kiss. A soft, tender caress that made Cass feel as if *she* was the one being comforted. He pulled her close against his chest, and she wrapped her arms around his shoulders and held on to him.

His tongue brushed against the seam of her lips, demanding entrance. She opened her mouth for him and was overwhelmed by Rafe's desire for her. He tasted of espresso and pumpkin pie, and Cass didn't want to ever let go. Rafe felt so solid, pressed next to her, that her earlier thoughts of isolation were ridiculous.

He was invincible. Cass realized that he didn't need her comfort. He was self-contained and preferred living that way.

Rafe's mouth left hers to trail along her cheek to her ear. He nibbled on the lobe before lifting his head. "Your mom didn't upset me."

Cass desperately needed to gather her thoughts. If her mom wasn't the problem then what was? Cass's stomach sank—the only answer was "her." "Did Andy let you watch the game in peace?"

"Yeah, he did." Cass heard the smile and wonder in his voice and wanted to smile with him.

"The word is *yes*, Rafe. I sometimes think your grammar is worse than Andy's."

"It probably is."

He smiled at her, and Cass thought that it was probably his first genuine happy expression of the day…except for that brief moment when he'd first entered the kitchen. But even that look had been tinged with a deep sadness.

"Would you like some help putting Andy to bed?" he asked.

"If you wouldn't mind. He's getting so big. I can't believe my baby's grown this fast. I remember—" She broke off, realizing that she was rambling. "You don't have to stay."

"I want to."

Cass wished he meant forever, but knew that it was only for the rest of the night. She told herself it didn't matter, but inside, her heart was breaking.

Rafe watched Cass move slowly around her son's bedroom. Andy slept the sleep of the innocent—something Rafe hadn't experienced in years. His own personal demons seemed to swarm closer at night, making sleep impossible. Over the years he'd accustomed himself to the feelings, but now his base instincts—like lust for a sweet lady—kept him up at night.

Cass bent to kiss Andy, and Rafe felt the butterfly caress on his own face. He remembered the scent of his mother's perfume as she brushed his hair back off his forehead and tucked the covers firmly around him. God, he missed her.

Holidays were hell, but today had been bearable, thanks to the Gambrels. Cass made it easy to relax in her home, easy to forget the memories and enjoy the day. Rafe liked being with Cass and her family. Too much.

Memories of his own family crept slowly into focus now that he was alone with his thoughts for the first time that evening. Cass was involved with tucking her son in. Damn, he was tired. He felt as if he carried a two-ton boulder on his shoulders.

Cass's son desperately wanted a father. Rafe bit back a groan of frustration. Mother and son were both so needy that he felt almost guilty spending time with them. He should leave them alone so that Cass could find a man who would be right for her. A decent nine-to-five guy, not a burnt-out construction worker with a past that wouldn't let him be.

Rafe left the boy's room. The domesticity of the scene

affected him more than he'd ever admit out loud. He
wanted to tell Cass that he would try to be whatever she
wanted. That he could be the man to complete her half-
formed family. That he'd be the man to fix the roof, mow
the lawn and help Andy grow into an adult who would be
respected by his peers.

Rafe went down the stairs and sat on the bottom step.
He wanted to, but couldn't. He couldn't be what she
wanted, and he couldn't risk hurting her and Andy. Much
as he wished it, there was no easy solution.

"Rafe, are you okay?"

Cass's voice was softer than the sun's first rays breaking
through night's hold on the sky. He glanced over his shoulder, catching his breath at the innate beauty of the woman
standing above him. She wasn't classically beautiful, some
might say she was only passing pretty, but to Rafe she was
the epitome of Woman—caring, firm, loving....

Love scared the hell out of him. He wasn't going to ride
that roller coaster again, he promised himself. No matter
how much he wanted Cass. "I'm fine, Cassie. Come on
down and we'll have that talk."

She opened her mouth as if to say something, but never
uttered a word. He knew how she felt. Afraid to move
forward with this strange relationship of theirs, yet afraid
to stay where they were and too weak to end it.

Dammit, why did life have to be so complicated? All
he'd wanted was a decent house and a yard where Tundra
could play outside. Instead he'd gotten a sexy, single
mother for a neighbor, and a little boy who desperately
needed adult-male guidance. Ah, hell...

He watched as she walked down. Cass had an innate
gracefulness. Most women slouched or moved in a hurry
but Cass always carried herself like a lady. Tonight Rafe
felt every rough edge he had, and there were a lot of them.
What did Cass see in him?

"Would you like some coffee?"

"No, thanks. Let's sit in here," he said, motioning to

the darkened living room. He'd spent the evening there imagining Cass sitting next to him on the soft leather sofa.

She perched beside him on the edge of the sofa and for a moment his only thought was of taking her in his arms. Physically he knew exactly what he wanted from Cass. Damn, he cursed silently.

His dreams last night had been filled with Cass on that bed he'd bought at the auction. The refinished piece now sat in the middle of his bedroom, but the bed felt empty without Cass in it with him.

He forced himself to relax against the back of the sofa, draping one arm around Cass. She sat stiffly for a moment before finally leaning against him. Rafe pretended not to notice how right she felt in his arms.

"Are you sure my mother didn't offend you?" she demanded.

"Will you please quit worrying about that?"

"I can't."

She was so solemn that he couldn't help laughing. "Oh, lady, what are we going to do?"

"Take it casually," she said with a soft sigh. She turned in his arms, placing her palm on his cheek. The contact burned straight through him to his groin. He wanted her, and if she didn't stop touching him, his control would shatter. "Although if you give me another nightgown like that red thing, I won't be responsible for my actions."

"Ah, hell, Cass. I think *casual* is out of the question for me."

"Why?"

Rafe's control was hair-trigger weak at the moment. Cass's breasts were pressed against his side, and that slim contact wasn't enough. He wanted more. Images of her in that sexy red gown he'd bought teased him. He wanted to see her wearing it and feel her responding to him in a way that only a certain man and his woman could. "I'll show you."

He lowered his head to kiss her. Her lips were soft and

sweet beneath his. He had to taste more of her. Thrusting his tongue into the velvety warmth of her mouth brought a groan of pure ecstasy to his throat.

She shifted restlessly against him, and Rafe lifted her to his lap. Her arms circled his shoulders, and the feel of her fingers in his hair reminded him of all he'd missed in the last few years. No other woman could ever compare to Cassandra Gambrel, he thought with awe.

Rafe let his hands roam down her slender back. Once again he was struck by how small and fragile she was. Her rump felt right cupped in his palms. She moved against him as if she enjoyed the contact as much as he did.

He burrowed his hands beneath her shirt. Her skin felt silky soft and made him want to howl his frustration to the moon. God, this woman was made for loving.

Slowly, because he knew he had to stop, and gently, because he knew that neither of them wanted to, he broke contact with her mouth and pulled his hands free of her clothing.

Cass's head rested on his shoulder with all the trust in the world. It amazed him that after his near-loss of control, she would still lie in his arms with all the faith of a devout believer. She should be rushing to get out of his embrace. She should be running for her life. Instead she sat there without a thought to her own self-preservation.

Then she moved closer. Her hips shifted against his groin in a way that made him want to adjust her legs and slide into her warmth. He could well imagine her body closing around him. She'd be hot and tight, and he'd go slowly out of his mind.

"Cassie, baby, get off my lap before I lose control."

She slid off his lap and stood. Rafe saw the tension, frustration and caring in her eyes. God, he wanted this woman.

"What now?" she asked, her voice stark with suppressed emotion.

"Is dating out of the question?" Rafe wanted to kick

himself. What was he thinking? He was supposed to be running for the hills, getting as far away from Cass and Andy as he could.

"No," she said softly. She brushed a tender kiss on his forehead. "I'd love to go out with you."

"Just you and me, Cass," he said, afraid that she didn't understand. "Two adults out on the town."

"Okay. I wouldn't have brought Andy along."

"Ah, hell, honey. I know that." Running had been his original intent, but damn, that woman made him feel good inside.

Cass leaned deeper into Rafe, trying to balance her hot chocolate. "Thanks for staying."

"It was the popcorn that decided me."

Cass heard the teasing note in his voice and knew that he wanted to watch this movie as much as she did. *Miracle on 34th Street* played softly in the background.

"Will you be disappointed if I tell you it came from the microwave?"

"No," he said, his mouth against her hair. Cass loved the way he could turn a simple, quiet evening into a special memory. She doubted either she or Andy would forget this Thanksgiving Day for a long time to come.

"I never realized how well made this movie is." He shifted his long legs, stretching them out across her lap.

Before she could protest the move, he lifted her and settled her length next to his. It was pleasantly comfortable, lying next to him like this. His hands swept down her back, and she knew he was trying to distract her. "You've never seen *Miracle* before."

He sighed into her hair. "Well, it's not exactly an action flick."

She watched his profile as he talked. He had a strong, classical-looking face. What had he said? Something about watching only action movies. "Is that your only criterion for watching a movie?"

"No, I think a good movie should have an athlete and a few good-looking women also."

Cass propped herself up on her elbow and glared down at him. "Raphael Santini, what would your mother say?"

The glitter in his eyes told her that her reaction was exactly what he'd hoped for.

"Probably the same thing you would."

"Do I remind you of her?" Cass asked, her voice sounding strained even to her own ears. She leaned down, resting her arms on his chest.

"You don't look like her," he said, thoughtfully.

Cass realized that Rafe wasn't upset by the comparison.

"It's the way you are with Andy and the caring you show for everyone that makes me think of my mom."

She sighed and snuggled closer to Rafe.

"You're sweet, Santini," she said the words lightly, knowing he'd deny the emotions of the moment.

"Ah, hell, Cassie."

"Don't cuss," she said softly. "Watch the movie. You're going to love this part."

She moved again on the couch, and Rafe shifted to his side, propping himself up behind her. One of his arms went around her waist and the other under her head. Cass ignored the movie and concentrated on the feeling of Rafe as he surrounded her.

His warmth surrounded her like the first ray of sun after a cold winter. She relaxed further into his body.

The evening was cool but not cold. Rafe had started a fire in the fireplace all the same. Now the scent of burning pine and the crackling of the fire lulled Cass to sleep.

She woke sometime before dawn. She was snuggled against Rafe's side, and he was snoring. How adorable, she thought. The man was physically perfect and had few flaws, but he snored.

She stared at his stubble-covered jaw, thinking about their talk the evening before. Where would this all lead?

To bed? To a life together? She didn't know, but she had to find out.

Her left arm was wedged under Rafe's head and painfully asleep. She cautiously freed her limb, and Rafe woke. He stared at her for a moment. "What time is it?"

His early-morning voice was rough, scratchy and even lower than normal. His eyes were staring at her lips and she wished he'd kiss her. Cass wet her lips, hoping to entice him.

He bent to nibble at her mouth for a moment before he stood. Rafe reached for her hand. "Walk me out."

She nodded and let him pull her to her feet.

"Will you go out with me on Saturday?" he asked, pausing at the door.

Cass smiled and then kissed him with all the tenderness his tousled form evoked. "I promised to take Andy fishing. I don't know when we'll get back."

"What do you know about fishing?"

Cass crossed her arms under her breasts and stared at him. "Nothing, but it can't be that hard."

Rafe laughed a deep, sexy sound that made Cass want to curl into his chest to absorb every nuance of the joyful expression.

"Want some company?"

"Are you an expert fisherperson?"

One eyebrow rose in that teasing way of his. Cass braced herself for some bit of humor. "I've caught more than I've let get away."

That sly dog…he thought that she would get flustered and blush. "Raphael G. Santini, what am I going to do with you?"

"Anything you want, baby. I'll pick you and Andy up at five o'clock Saturday morning. Dress sexy," he said with a wink.

Cass laughed out loud as he walked away. Rafe always had to have the last word. Then the reality of what he said sank in. Five o'clock, *in the morning!* She groaned before going back inside the house.

# Eight

**T**he early-morning fog cleared away to reveal the bright fall sun. Rafe smothered a yawn beneath his hand and sank deeper into his boat chair. Andy was wide awake and had been excitedly reeling in bass all morning.

There was something calming and peaceful about being on the water this early in the day. The boat rocked soothingly as Rafe scanned the nearly empty lake. Only one other boat bobbed in the distance, far enough away to appear as only a speck.

Fishing and hunting brought out the elemental man in him. It was probably some Neanderthal gene that reveled in the masculine joy of bringing in fresh game from the hunt—providing for the family. Andy seemed to be basking in the same glow. Rafe felt his chest expand with pride as he watched Cass's son. The boy was slowly working his way into Rafe's heart and there wasn't a damn thing he could do about it.

Cass would in no way ever be an expert on fishing. She

was still trying to bait her hook. She looked adorable with her large sunglasses and her floppy clothing. But he'd felt the strong, feminine body underneath, so the baggy clothing teased his imagination.

"Want some help?" he asked, drawling the question in a teasing manner.

"No," she said.

Cass was stubborn. The lady refused to accept defeat. Rafe didn't doubt that she and Andy would've had a successful fishing expedition without him. Cass would settle for nothing less.

"I have a fly hook you can use."

"Rafe," she said, in that sobering mother tone she used when Andy was misbehaving. "If I can't get this darn worm on the hook, what makes you think a fly would be easier?"

He laughed, earning himself a sharp glare from Cass and a conspiratorial grin from Andy. "Let me show you how. No one comes out their first time and baits their own hook."

"Thanks for trying to make me feel better, but even I'm not that gullible." She looked so cute standing there at the back of the boat in the floppy fishing hat he'd given her this morning.

"Hell, honey. I'm not boosting your ego—that's the truth." Andy's grin took up his entire face as he watched his mom. Rafe winked at the boy.

"Don't cuss," she said, but her heart wasn't in the reprimand.

Rafe glanced at her in disbelief. Cass was taking fishing much too seriously. Women weren't meant for the sport, he thought, they didn't get the same primal rush men did.

"Andy?" he asked, hoping his new bond with the boy extended to mind reading. Cass needed her spirits boosted and Rafe knew the perfect way to do it.

"Yeah?"

"It's yes." They corrected Andy at the same time. Cass

looked at him and Rafe shrugged. He didn't know where that had come from. To cover his awkwardness he asked Andy, "Did you bait your hook the first time you went fishing?"

"No, my dad did it for me. Want me to show you how, Mom?"

"No thanks, sweetie." Cass's smile was bittersweet as she set the pole aside and hugged her son. She plopped the fishing hat on Andy's head. "We don't want you to get sunburned."

Andy grimaced but left the hat in place, before returning to the bow of the boat. He cast his line expertly, apparently assured that his mom would be okay.

"You have to coax the worm onto the hook, Cass."

"I'm trying," she said breathlessly. Her voice, soft and frustrated, brushed over his nerve endings like wildfire through dry timber.

Rafe checked Andy's position at the bow of the boat before walking to Cass. He stood behind her, staring at the slender line of her back. She was a strong woman, but at the same time fragile.

Part of him, the masculine Neanderthal part, liked that. He liked thinking of her as weaker and needing him to defend her, protect her and provide for her. Rafe grimaced as he thought of what Cass's reaction to those thoughts would be. She'd probably push his Neanderthal butt in the water.

The sun brought out the reddish-brown highlights in her thick hair, making it shimmer like a forbidden treasure. He wanted, no, *needed* to bury his hands in the thick mass of curling hair. To feel a part of her wrapped around him, to pretend for a moment that he was a part of her.

He forced his hands to hers instead and helped her adjust her grip on the hook. "Coax the worm gently, like you would a lover. Tease it softly until it gets on the hook of its own free will. Slowly…"

Beneath his fingers, he felt Cass tense. He altered his

position behind her and pulled her firmly into the cradle of his body. A rush of desire hit him broadside as the sweet scent that was uniquely Cass surrounded him.

Cass tried once again, but the worm refused to go on the hook. "I *will* do this."

"Relax, honey. You're rushing. Take it slow and easy." As he spoke Rafe rubbed his forefinger over her wrist and slowly Cass relaxed.

Rafe battled down his base needs and wrapped his arms gently around Cass. He heard the emotion underlying her words and knew that she saw her inability to bait the hook as a failing. He lowered his head brushing his lips against her neck. A shiver coursed through her, inciting a fire in his senses.

Cass's hands shook. "You're not helping." The tart words were softened by the husky timbre of her voice.

"I'm trying to." He tried to pretend that he didn't notice the soft, pressure of her back and buttocks pressed into his chest and groin, but didn't succeed. Damn, he wanted her.

His body was tight and aching—he needed Cass more than he needed his next breath. And there wasn't a damn thing he could do about it at that moment.

"Ah, hell," he muttered beneath his breath and felt Cass stiffen.

"Don't cuss," she admonished.

"Lady, you're making me crazy."

Her head dropped, and she muttered something so soft he couldn't make out the words. She shoved the hook toward the worm in her hand and speared the fleshy part of her palm. The small nick didn't bleed but Rafe knew it had to hurt.

"Stubborn woman." Rafe put his hands over Cass's and smoothly hooked the worm. He dropped the line over the side of the boat and propped her pole up before bringing her injured hand to his lips.

He brushed the small abrasion with his tongue. Rafe bit back a curse as she curved her fingers around his jaw, holding him to her. He took one last taste before stepping away. This wasn't the time or place for that type of play.

Cass stared up at him. "Why?"

Rafe didn't need clarification he knew what she was asking. He was asking himself the same damn question. Maybe it was the same Neanderthal gene. All he knew was that he wanted to wrap his hands around those sweetly curved hips of hers and toss her over his shoulder. He gritted his teeth against the need to actually carry her away from here and back to his bedroom. Hell, any quiet, private place would do.

Dammit! He wasn't some big, dumb, macho jock. He knew how to act like a sophisticated gentleman. Why did Cass always make him forget that? Around her he was the most elemental of men. Acting on hormonal impulses instead of logic.

Cass was still staring up at him with those wide, gingery eyes of hers that made him feel like a creep for thinking these things. Especially when she hadn't done anything to tempt him. It wasn't her fault that she was everything he wanted and at the same time a woman he should not have.

"Stupidity," he said, before stalking to the bow of the boat to sit with Andy.

"Rafe?"

He stopped but didn't look back. He knew that one more second of close contact with her and he wouldn't be able to resist the temptation of her lips. Then he'd want to explore her mouth at leisure. He had to stop thinking of sex with every breath he took.

"I'm...thanks for helping with the worm."

Always polite no matter how crass he was to her. Always a damn lady, and he was nothing more than a rough, Italian construction worker. "No problem."

He hurried to Andy, hoping the small boy would take his mind off of the sexy lady sitting quietly at the back of the boat.

* * *

Thunderclouds threatened rain, and Rafe didn't want to panic Andy or Cass, but he had a bad feeling niggling the back of his neck. "Pull in your lines. We're getting out of here."

"What's wrong?" Cass asked.

In her eyes he saw the trust she had in him. She wanted to be aware of any problems, even though she knew he could handle them. Rafe liked the feeling. "Nothing yet. But the sky's darkening."

Cass nodded in understanding. "Hurry up, son."

Andy reeled in his empty line and quietly set about putting away his gear. Cass moved a bit more quickly, settling herself and Andy onto the bench in the back of the boat.

"Put on your life jackets," Rafe said.

They all donned the bright orange jackets before Rafe started the boat. He wanted to open the throttle and hurry them across the lake and through the connecting chain to the next one, but the water was choppy. The boat bounced like a yo-yo, out of control even at half throttle. A glance at the sky told him to chance rocking the boat and he gradually increased their speed.

"Is everything okay?" Cass asked from his shoulder.

"I'm worried about that thundercloud over there." He pointed out to the horizon.

"It looks like a funnel cloud," she said. "I think we should get off the water."

"I know. Go sit back down with Andy."

"Can we make it to that dock?" she asked, pointing to an abandoned boathouse on the distance shore.

"I'm going to try."

But the winds picked up and the heavens opened. They were drenched in a matter of minutes. Rafe banked sharply, heading for the boathouse Cass had selected. By the time they reached the dock, the wind was buffeting around them. Cass's face was white with worry, and Andy held on tightly to his mother.

Rafe knew that only activity would get the boy's mind off of his fear. "Andy, I need your help."

The little boy straightened, moving away from his mother. "What can I do?"

"You and your mom tie up the boat when we get inside the boathouse."

In a short while the boat was secured and they were seated in the darkened boathouse. The structure wasn't much, but at least it provided shelter from the storm.

"Andy, are you okay?" Cass asked.

"I'm fine, Mom. Can I go play in the boat?"

"Rafe?"

"It should be safe."

"Okay."

Rafe scooted closer to Cass and wrapped an arm around her shoulders. "Don't worry, honey. I won't let anything happen to you or Andy."

"I know," she said.

It hit Rafe then, that he'd done exactly what he'd said he wouldn't do. He'd committed himself to this small family and started caring about them. Hell, he more than cared for them. He was beginning to love them.

# Nine

Love. Rafe stopped that thought before it was fully formed. He didn't have the capacity to love. He doubted any of the lighter emotions had survived his parents' deaths. The few that had were killed when his sister passed away only weeks later.

The guilt he'd felt at having not been there for his family that night had eliminated any dreams he'd had of one day having a wife and child of his own. Rafe felt more at fault than the wet, slick road.

This protective desire for Cass came damn close to feelings he'd hoped to have forgotten. He'd forgotten about the softer emotions—how they wrapped themselves snugly around his soul and made his heart ache.

He didn't like remembering now. He especially didn't want to love a woman like Cass—a woman who'd want more than his body. He'd never been in love with a woman before—he'd been in lust more times than a gentleman should be, but never in love.

And it scared the hell out of him.

This wasn't love. It was probably just a bad case of...what? It felt more intense than lust because there was more longing in his soul than just for her body. He wanted to be with her constantly. He wanted her caring, her kindness, her sense of humor and her innate dignity. No woman had ever tempted him on so many different levels before.

The past few years had been an emotional wasteland, and Cass drew him to her with the promise of a safe home to rest and rejuvenate his weary soul. But he knew it wasn't love he was feeling. He wouldn't allow himself to be that weak, that vulnerable, again.

He shifted away from Cass, feeling trapped—by her presence and the storm. He wished he were at home so that he could climb behind the wheel of his Jag. He would race down the highway until the wind ripped away all of his thoughts and feelings. He'd race until the only thing he felt was fatigue. He'd race so far and fast that his emotions would never be able to catch up to him.

He needed to move, to pace the length of the small, wooden boathouse. But Cass chose that moment to put her hand on his thigh. Her touch burned through him like a strike of white lightning on dry timberland. The sexual desire that was always under the surface when he was close to Cass flared to life.

His cutoffs were too tight—he blamed that fact on his active imagination. He lifted her hand from his leg and placed it back on her own. Cass slid her arm around his waist and rested her head on his chest, right above his heart. Damn, but the woman made it hard not to care about her.

Cass shivered and burrowed closer to him. He was amazed at the easy way she always reached for him. She'd lost the man she loved, yet she was willing, almost eager to try again.

Her body felt so sweet curled up against him. The floral smell of her perfume had diluted after a morning spent in the sun, but the essence of Cass was still there. A soft, feminine scent that reminded him of family and home.

It was dark in the boathouse, and Rafe lowered his nose to the top of her head and inhaled deeply. He cursed silently under his breath calling himself ten kinds of fool.

He straightened, but Cass looked up at him. Her eyes wide with fear and another less-easily defined emotion. He wanted her to be safe...to feel protected.

"What is it?" she asked.

Rafe was amazed that she could read his moods so easily. He settled back beside her, not wanting her to worry. And Cass would worry.

That was the type of woman she was. She had a maternal instinct larger than the state of Texas and showered it on anyone she cared about. Already Cass was more intuitive to his moods than any other person. She'd know something was wrong and he couldn't explain to her what his feelings were.

"Rafe?"

He heard the hesitancy, the doubt and the fear in her voice, but there wasn't a damn thing he could say to reassure her. The storm outside would continue to roar until it was good and ready to stop. It seemed to be gathering intensity. "We'll be okay."

Yeah, right. His emotions would continue to churn and boil out of control until he stopped them. And he couldn't stop them by sleeping with Cass. Not the way he felt about her.

Making love to her would be too intense and too revealing. He would have no protective layers left, once he was sheathed in her body. He'd be so damn vulnerable. There was no way he could do it.

The walls closed in around him, and Rafe stood. He was halfway to the boat before he remembered he couldn't leave. A small boy and his mother were depending on him. He pivoted on his heel and saw the two of them huddled together, watching him nervously.

Rafe was so caught up in his own introspection that he'd missed Andy's retreat to his mom. Each roll of thunder pounded through the boathouse, threatening to topple the ill-constructed building with the sheer loudness of the sound. The storm crackled and roared outside, frightening both Gambrels. Mother and son needed him.

"Rafe, are you okay?" Cass asked again.

"Yes, I'm a bit claustrophobic." Liar, his subconscious jeered. You're a bit foolish. "Let's try to find something to take our minds off the storm."

"I wish I had my Nintendo," Andy said.

In his voice was the fear that the seven-year-old would never admit to having. It was a man thing, Rafe decided, because he sure as hell wouldn't admit to being scared, either. Not of the storm and not of the softer emotions stirring to life inside his forgotten soul.

"Me too, pal."

Andy's smile hit him broadside, and Rafe absorbed the fact that nothing would make him not care and worry about this family. He needed to distract everyone from the rising storm. But how?

If he and Cassie were alone, they would pass the time by coming to terms with the explosive desire that was blossoming between them. Exploring and devouring each other. But Andy's presence ruled that option out. Besides, there was more to his relationship with Cass than heat and passion.

"Let's play twenty questions," Cass suggested, her voice quavering a little as she spoke.

"No."

"Why not?"

"It's too involved." And he didn't want to have to answer a slew of personal questions now. The disappointment in Cass's eyes made his heart ache. Though she'd probably never admit it, the silence had gotten to her.

"Besides, I haven't any secrets, except for my middle name." He knew that Cass still wanted to know what it was. She'd asked him several times over the past few days about it. Casually she'd bring up the subject and always she had an unique name for him.

"Okay," Cass said.

"Is it Peter?" Andy asked.

"No, honey," Cass said before he could answer. "It starts with a *G*."

"Is it Gary?"

"No, it's ethnic." Rafe watched mother and son look at each other. Andy was more intelligent than the average seven-year-old. Rafe had a feeling that before long the mother-son team would uncover his hated middle name. There simply weren't that many Italian names that started with the letter *G*. "I'm only giving you each one guess."

"I don't know many Italian names," Andy said. "Is it Giovanni?"

"No," Rafe said with a shake of his head. "Cass?"

"Guiseppi?"

Rafe burst out laughing.

"Am I right?"

"No, but you're close."

"May I have another guess?" Andy asked. "I know Mom's been guessing for weeks."

"How do you know that?" Rafe was curious. It didn't seem like the type of thing Cass would tell her son. He glanced at Cass and saw that she was blushing. Even in the faint light, he could see the color sweeping down her neck.

Rafe had never considered kids a source of truth, but was reconsidering that. He'd learned more about Cass from her son than from anyone else. He remembered the first morning they'd met and Andy's telling words. *The one you said had cute buns.*

"Mom dug out the Bible last night and was searching for saint names."

"Cassie," he said in a wondering tone. "I had no idea."

"Don't take it too seriously. I wanted to read ahead for next week's sermon at church."

"Did the Good Book help with the name search?"

"No, but the Italian name book yielded several ideas."

Rafe laughed out loud. He hadn't felt this good in years. Cass and Andy laughed along with him, and for the first time since that horrible car crash he felt part of a family. He wallowed in the closeness, knowing it wouldn't last, but enjoying it just the same.

"What can we do next?" Andy asked.

"Nothing," Rafe said. Sometime during their game, the storm had lessened. "I'm going outside to check on the storm."

"Can I come with you?" Andy asked.

Rafe really needed the time alone to come to terms with his emotions and feelings, but Andy's face was so hopeful. He hadn't forgotten what it was like to have a bad case of hero worship, and though being the idol was new to Rafe, the emotions on the other end weren't. "Cass?"

"Sure, but be careful."

"Aw, Mom, of course we'll be careful."

Cass dropped a kiss on her son's forehead, pushing him toward the door. Rafe followed the small boy, but Cass's hand on his wrist stopped him. She stood on her toes and brushed a kiss against his jaw. "You be careful, too."

Rafe walked outside thinking that he didn't know a damn thing about pain. True torment was seeing what you wanted but knowing if you reached out and grabbed it, it would all disappear quicker than a snowflake in hell.

Cass dropped Andy off at her mom's house on Saturday afternoon. Rafe had seen them safely home, but the burning promise in his eyes told her he was eagerly anticipating their date. Her son was sleepy, but excited to see his aunt Sara, Cass's younger sister, who was home on vacation.

Cass's mom told her to have a good time, but Sara told her to be careful. "Santini doesn't seem like a reckless man, but there's no sense in not protecting yourself."

Cass opened the car door before glancing back at her

sister. Sara was the closest thing the Gambrels had to a black sheep. Still single at the age of twenty-six and no prospects for a husband. So Cass knew the advice Sara was dishing out couldn't be said in front of their mom.

"What are you talking about? Rafe would never hurt me."

Sara rolled her eyes and sighed like a parent talking to a backward child. "Pregnancy, Cass. Don't tell me you've forgotten how Andrew got here? I know you're not on the pill. Stop on the way home and buy some condoms."

Sara's words haunted her as she drove back home. Surely Rafe would take care of that. But what if he didn't? She really didn't want to be waiting and worrying over whether or not she was pregnant. She and Rafe had enough strikes against having a lasting relationship without adding that worry to the pile.

She turned into the Wal-Mart parking lot before she'd realized it. She sat in the car for five minutes before deciding to go inside. Cass walked into the discount department store and grabbed a cart. She forced herself to act calmly and not glance furtively over her shoulder as if she were a criminal.

Teenage boys buy these things all the time, she assured herself. Even teenage girls. She pushed the cart past the drug and hygiene section and spent fifteen minutes looking at pool supplies before she returned to the pharmacy.

She tried to look casual as she made a left turn down the aisle. The contraceptives were on the end of the aisle right in front of the pharmacist's counter. Cass supposed that was to discourage kids from buying them.

She glanced quickly at the shelf, figuring that she would just grab one package. She was surprised to see so much variety. There were contraceptives for men and women. There was a gel, a sponge and plain old rubbers. There was more here than she knew what to do with.

Which one should she buy? She heard another buggy turn down the aisle and blindly reached out grabbing some of everything. She tossed the packages into the cart and pushed her way around the corner.

Her face felt red and she wondered how the heck she was ever going to pay for them. She really wanted to take the time to read the boxes and make sure she was buying the right product. Oh, well, she thought, better to just get out of here. She could read them at home, in privacy.

She maneuvered her way to the checkout counter. She piled the boxes neatly on the counter and hoped the girl would ring them up quickly. The girl did, without a word, which made Cass wonder if everyone bought several different types of contraceptives.

Cass drove all the way home wondering if she was doing the right thing. But in her heart there were no worries. She loved Rafe.

Cass stared at Rafe as they waited for the valet to bring their car around. Dinner had been a slow, sophisticated affair, and Cass was looking forward to relaxing in the car with Rafe. She'd been afraid to talk about anything personal in the restaurant.

Her pulse jumped at the thought of the coming night. She couldn't wait to be in his arms, to feel his skin against hers, to become one with him. She tried to convince herself that she wasn't ruled by her hormones, but had a hard time of it.

For the first time in her life she wished she were anyone else but Cassandra Lynn Gambrel. She wished she were sophisticated and glamorous. Rafe deserved to have a woman on his arm who could match him in style. Not a single mother with the fashion sense of a Victorian spinster.

She wished she'd pulled out that Jane Fonda tape that had been collecting dust since Andrew's birth and that she'd spent more time exercising and less time eating baked goods.

She wished she could be what he needed—what she knew he was looking for even though he wouldn't acknowledge that he was looking. She sighed, wiping her sweaty palm on the skirt of her dress.

Cass couldn't help staring at Rafe as he tipped the valet. She couldn't believe that this man was out with her—that he felt even a smidgen of what she did, and that she'd inspired that feeling in him.

"Come on, baby. Let's go home."

Cass shivered at the thought and let him help her into the car. He didn't say a word as he piloted them out of the parking lot and onto the highway.

The night sky was filled with stars, and a cool breeze blew in through the open top of the car. Rafe drove with the ease and certainty of a confident man.

He kept his eyes on the road, but his right hand left the wheel to rest on her thigh. His fingers stroked her leg through the cloth, and Cass felt the electricity of his touch go through her. She reached for his hand linking their fingers.

He tried to free his hand, but she held tight. She didn't want to feel the intense physical desire that Rafe evoked in her while they were driving down the street. She shivered at the heat in his gaze as he glanced over at her.

"Relax, baby. We'll be home soon."

Cass forced herself to relax into the leather seats, forgetting to worry about the thousands of doubts that had been assailing since she left the Wal-Mart parking lot.

"I promised you an evening full of surprises. And I intend to deliver."

Rafe was behaving oddly tonight. For the first time she felt as if she were facing a stranger instead of a flesh-and-blood man. He was dressed fashionably in a Brooks Brothers suit and silk tie. He'd behaved during dinner with the sophistication of a connoisseur. He'd ordered wine from the sommelier with knowledgeable assurance, and had rattled off the names of French dishes as if he were Parisian.

Another telling sign was the music. Rafe usually played loud, raunchy country music and sang boldly at the top of his lungs. Tonight, he put a CD in the player that was a stylish, jazz instrumental, which was slowly giving her a headache.

Cass had the sudden realization that Rafe wasn't planning on enjoying the evening and getting to know her. He was planning on seducing her, using a cold-blooded, calculated set of moves. That made her angry. She could handle the fact that he didn't want a long-term commitment from her, but she'd be damned if she'd let him treat her like some one-night stand, like some woman he'd picked up for an evening's delight.

She deserved better treatment and so did he. "I think you'd better drop me at home," she said as he pulled into his driveway.

Rafe didn't say a word, but shut off the car and glanced at her. "Why?"

"You're not enjoying this evening," she said stiffly, and reached for the door handle.

"I plan to," he said, giving her another one of those hot looks of his. He grabbed her hand and brought it to his lips, kissing and nipping at each of her fingers in turn. Cass felt a warm, melting sensation—the onslaught of desire rushing through her veins—but she didn't give in. She knew that she'd never been ruled by her hormones, and she wasn't about to start now.

"No, thanks, Rafe. I want to be with a man who's enjoying my company as much as I'm enjoying his."

"I am enjoying your company." He leaned over to kiss her. Cass felt the cool calculation in him, even as she responded to the temptation he offered. A few seconds passed before she forced herself to move away from him.

"No, you're too busy concentrating on seducing me. I thought I knew you, but I guess I was wrong."

He didn't say anything, but Cass knew he was waiting for her to explain. "The man I've come to know dresses for comfort, not fashion, and he listens to raunchy, loud music, not sophisticated jazz."

"I thought you liked jazz," he said.

Cass noticed that he didn't contradict the fact that he didn't like the music he'd been forcing on them all evening. "That's not the point."

"What is?"

"I feel like you're not at all here. Like you've put your body on autopilot and gone into seduction mode. I want you, Rafe, but I also care about you. I'm not ready to be a one-night stand—not even with you."

She quietly opened the door and glanced back at him. He sat silently as if weighing her words. "I had a nice time at dinner."

Cass walked away without looking back. She thought of the contraceptives in her purse and the disappointment she was now feeling. She felt like crying, but wouldn't let herself.

"Cassie?"

She stopped. It was the first time that evening Rafe had called her anything but "baby."

"Yes?"

"Please stay."

# Ten

Cass didn't leave, but she made no move to go back to him. For the first time that evening, Rafe doubted its conclusion. He doubted himself and his reasons for wanting this woman in his bed. He doubted the honesty he'd always expected from himself. But he didn't doubt his feelings for Cass.

He'd expected her to come to his bed as easily as women in the past had. His Casanova ways had always served him well, but with this one woman they hadn't worked at all. He didn't blame her for trying to leave, but he wasn't going to let her go. He couldn't allow her to slip through his fingers, not when he'd come so close to finding something that had been missing in his life—in his soul.

"Cassie, I'm sorry. I'm…" Scared, he thought, but knew he couldn't admit it.

Cass walked back to him, staring up at him in the dim light of the evening. She stood so close he could feel the heat of her body, smell her sweet scent and breathe her breath. But still a distance remained between that would be hard to bridge.

"Are you nervous, Rafe?"

In her voice were a hundred unasked questions, and he heard them all in his mind. He wanted to avoid answering, but he knew that she would walk out of his life forever if he did.

*Was* he nervous? He'd applied many terms to himself that evening and *nervous* hadn't been one of them. He shrugged. "I don't know."

He couldn't shake the feeling of expectancy that settled over his body like a cloak. But then again, he'd never wanted to make love to a woman. He'd desired a lot of women and taken dozens to bed, but he'd never really made love to anyone.

"Maybe I am nervous," he said softly. He never examined his emotions unless forced to, preferring to drift through life without knowing how others affected him, but he knew Cass. She needed to put labels on her emotions and on his, to understand why they each reacted the way that they did with each other.

"*I'm* nervous," she said with a shaky sigh. He thought she might be near tears, but that was a characteristic he never associated with Cass. "And scared and unsure, but I'm willing to—"

"Don't, Cassie," he said, hearing her voice crack. He blamed himself for every one of her fears, hurts and doubts. He wrapped her in a big bear hug and held her. "Don't tear yourself up because I'm a bastard."

"You're not," she said.

Again she rested directly over his heart, making him feel like she had moved in there. She felt so damn right that the last thing he ever wanted to do was let her go.

"Ready to go inside?" he asked, after several minutes had passed.

She nodded, and they walked up the path to his front

door with their arms around each other. Inside, the house
was dark and welcoming.

Rafe bit back a primeval roar of satisfaction. Cass was
in his home. Under his arm she felt soft and womanly, and
he longed to claim her. But she was still tense, and he was
to blame for that. He decided to stall for time and try to
regain his control and her trust.

"I'll be right back," he said. He went down the hall to
the kitchen. Rafe grabbed a bottle of wine from the refrigerator, remembering the first night he'd kissed Cass. She'd
been so sure that he would walk out of her life. Hell, so
had he.

He remembered the warm, honeyed taste of her mouth,
the soft brush of her breasts against his chest and the way
his soul felt as if he'd come home. Damn, it wasn't working.

His body tightened in response to his thoughts. All he
could think of was having those long legs of hers wrapped
around his hips, her breasts under his hands and lips and
her heart beating wildly in time with his. He groaned out
loud, sure that the next time he saw Cass he'd take her
where they stood.

"Rafe?"

He didn't want to turn around and look at her. What if
she still seemed vulnerable and scared? God, he was such
a brute. First he treated her like someone he just picked up
for the night, and then he left her alone in the living room.
Making *love* to a woman was a lot more difficult than he'd
thought. There was more than sexual technique involved
here.

"Rafe?"

She stood in the doorway leading to the hall. She'd removed her shoes, and Rafe found her bare feet extremely
attractive. Her long legs were encased in nylon, and he
wondered if she wore a garter belt. For a moment all he
could think about was touching her legs.

He held the open bottle of wine in one hand and two

stemmed wineglasses in the other. "Are you thirsty?" he asked.

She shook her head. Her purse was clutched to her stomach, and he wondered why she hadn't left it in the living room with her shoes. He guessed the nerves she spoke of earlier still bothered her and it was up to him to rid her of that tension.

"Come on," he said, grabbing her hand and leading her up the stairs to the bedroom. "I want you to see the bed. I've pictured you in here a thousand times."

"I had a few thoughts of you in that bed while I was working on it," she confessed shyly.

Cass, he reminded himself again, wasn't used to sleeping with a man who wasn't her husband. If fact, he doubted she'd slept with more than one man in her entire life. He suddenly felt more than a little nervous. Cass deserved so much more than he could give her.

But she was looking at him with desire and hope in her ginger-colored eyes. She was counting on him to help her through this. He grimaced at the thought, as if making love were a chore. He decided they both needed some humor to lighten the moment. "I'd rather you work on me."

"Oh, Rafe. I'm so glad you're back to being you."

She laughed and the joyful sound followed him into his room. The moon cast a dim light across the shadow, clearly showing the conflicting emotions on her face. "Why?"

"Because you're more approachable this way."

"Do you want to approach me?" he asked, in a deep voice. He felt more secure now than he'd ever felt before with her. Cass was finally where she belonged, in his bedroom. But part of him refused to believe she'd stay. He tugged her purse from her hands and tossed it toward the nightstand.

He pulled her into his arms. God, she felt right there. Bending, he dropped a dozen small kisses across her face and the bridge of her nose. The taste was addictive, and he continued nibbling on her skin.

Her hands burrowed under his jacket and rubbed up and down the length of his back. He moaned deep in his throat, wanting more of her touch. She slid her hands into the back of his pants, running her nails along the border of his back and buttocks.

"Like that?" she asked with a teasing note in her voice. Cass for all her shyness was a sensual person. She caressed her way around to the front of his body and up to his shoulders before toying with the knot of his tie. "How about if I take this off for you?"

"Go for it, babe."

She stiffened but didn't pull away. "Don't call me babe or baby."

He nibbled on her bottom lip. "Why not?"

She freed her mouth from his. "Because you call every woman that."

"I don't," he said, running his hands down her torso. The dress she was wearing was ingeniously designed and the zipper well hidden. At last he found it and tugged it down, peeling the fabric apart as he went.

The skin of her back was smooth as silk and rippled under his touch. The lace border on her slip felt rough and coarse compared with her flesh. He ran his thumb along the seam down her spine, enjoying the sensual shiver that coursed through her body. This woman was a delight to love. Her body fit his perfectly, and for the moment that was all that mattered.

He lowered her to the bed, bringing his mouth to hers. The kiss was hot, deep and a promise of what was to come. He thrust his tongue past the barrier of her teeth and reveled in the possessive feeling that swamped him. *Cass was his.*

She freed his tie from his shirt and started in on the buttons. Rafe couldn't wait to get that damned dress off her. He longed to feel her naked skin against his.

The touch of her fingers made him groan out loud. She traced a path down the center of his chest, stopping at his belt buckle.

Rafe wanted to be doing the same to her. He peeled the dress off her body and pulled back to stare. Cass was finely made. Though she'd had a child, no evidence remained on her stomach. It was flat and firm.

The lacy cups of her bra hugged her curves, and Rafe reached beneath her to undo the clasp. He tugged away the last piece of clothing on her upper body. He rubbed his chest against the tips of her breasts. The light pink nipples felt damn good touching his skin.

"Cassie, you're beautiful," he said. He bent his head to tongue her nipples, which immediately hardened under his mouth, begging for a deeper caress. He nibbled his way around each of her breasts before taking her nipple into his mouth and sucking gently. Her hips rose from the bed pressing into him.

Rafe rubbed his groin against her soft, womanly mound. He felt the pleasure of that contact rush through his body like leaves caught up in the wind. Passion took over completely.

He reached down to caress her moist heat through the fabric of her panties. She writhed against him as he bent to suckle at her breasts again. When Cass touched him through his pants, he thought he'd explode then and there.

"Rafe..."

He fumbled at his belt buckle eager to be naked and join with Cass.

"Uh, Rafe..." she said, her hands holding his still in the fastenings of his pants.

"What?" If she asked him to stop now, he'd kill himself. He honestly didn't think that he could.

"I have something for you."

"I have something for you too," he said with a wicked chuckle. "But you have to let go of my hands first."

"Not that." Cass flushed.

He brushed his fingers over her breasts as the blush spread down her neck. She shivered against his touch and sighed. She wasn't going to ask him to stop, he thought, but something was on her mind. With an effort he controlled his desire and asked, "Where is this gift?"

"In my purse."

He bent and picked her bag up from the floor. He knew then what Cass wanted to give him. The love he'd thought to control and conceal blossomed in his heart. He knew then that he'd always love this woman.

"Oh, this is so embarrassing." She reached for the purse and pulled out a box of condoms and some sort of woman's contraceptive Rafe had never seen before.

"Don't be embarrassed," he said, taking the unopened boxes from her. "Be proud that you had the courage to take the initiative here. But we don't need your gift. I have my own." He opened the nightstand drawer and removed a foil packet. He leaned down to cover her body again and murmured, "We'll save yours for the next time."

He kissed her then, with all the tenderness that had been welling up inside of him since he'd met her. He kissed like there was no tomorrow and this night would never end. He kissed her the way a man kisses the woman he loves.

He stood to remove the rest of their clothing. Then lay next to her on the bed. The old mattress seemed to welcome the lovers, embracing them. Cass rested her head over his heart and her hand on his chest. Rafe enjoyed the full body contact and the gentle moment for as long as he could. But desire reared its formidable head, and passion demanded more of them both.

His hands swept up and down her back enjoying the soft curves and tempting hollows of her body. Cass made him revel in being a man. Never before had he felt the urge to explore a woman completely—no matter how long it took.

He slid his palm down the flat expanse of her stomach and teased the flesh around her belly button. She giggled and returned the caress.

"Stop tickling," she said, biting his ear in response.

He let his fingers move lower to the flower of her womanhood. He stroked and petted until he knew she was ready for him. He slid the condom into place on his own body and positioned himself over her.

"Cassie?" he asked, needing to be sure this was what she wanted.

"Now, Rafe. Please."

He tried to go slowly, but she was so damn tight and felt so good wrapped around him. He lifted her legs, and she locked them around his waist, the way he'd imagined she would, but better. He plunged into her again and again until they both plummeted over the edge of oblivion. He heard her calling his name and echoed with hers as he climaxed.

He ignored the part of his soul that felt as if he had found his mate. He was meant to remain alone for the rest of this life, but she felt so right under him and around him that he held her close. He squeezed his eyes shut and pretended that this hadn't changed the course of his life.

Cass woke a couple of hours later. There was no moment of not knowing where she was or who she was with. She'd recognize those strong arms wrapped around her anyplace and anytime, she thought, snuggling closer to him. His heart beat strongly under her cheek, and the scent of their loving lingered in the air. Never before had she felt this close to another person.

She sighed and rubbed her fingers through the coarse hair covering his chest. She wondered if he was going to continue sleeping. She started to slide slowly back to sleep, when she realized that she would have to leave his house before morning.

What if one of the neighbors saw her? Oh, no, why hadn't she thought of this sooner? Worse than any neighbor's opinion was Rafe's. What if their lovemaking had been no different than any of his past affairs? What if she meant no more to him than a night's fleeting pleasure?

"Cassie?"

She glanced down at Rafe. His eyes were half-opened, his hands were on hers, removing her nails from his chest.

She'd unintentionally dug them into his skin while her mind dwelled on a hundred worries.

"What's wrong, honey?"

"Nothing. I..." Cass figured nothing could be more embarrassing than buying condoms, but was once again flushed with emotion. "I don't know what to do or say. Should I leave now? Should I stay? Dammit, the etiquette books never covered situations like this."

"What do you want to do?" he asked, laughing. His arms held her close, and though he teased her, she still sensed the tension in his prone figure. She'd been trying to think of a polite answer, but she realized Rafe deserved her honesty.

The scared, shy part of her wanted to run, but she knew he wouldn't let her. Rafe was an immovable force when he wanted to be. She thought about the easy way she'd dealt with Carl. He had let her have her way most of the time. Rafe Santini wasn't like that. He wouldn't let her manipulate him.

"I don't know," she finally admitted, and tore her eyes from his. How could she tell him what she was feeling, when he was staring at her with such a fierce...hunger? "I like your arms around me."

He sighed and then brushed a kiss against her shoulder. "Stay. Sleep with me through the night and into the morning."

*Rafe wanted her to stay with him.* She felt blissful, joyful....

"What about the neighbors?"

He rolled over, pinning her beneath him. "What about them? Cass, you're an adult. It's none of their business what you do."

"Rafe, I'm serious. I don't want Andy to be subject to nasty rumors about his sex-starved, widowed mother. I don't want people saying—"

Rafe covered her mouth with his hand. She stared at him for a moment, then closed her eyes. This was humiliating.

He probably thought the same thing her neighbors would think, that she'd jumped into bed with the first available man to pay her the least bit of attention. She wanted to die.

He removed his hand from her mouth, but she refused to open her eyes. What had she been thinking to say those words out loud? She felt the gentle brush of his breath across her lips a millisecond before his lips touched hers.

His lips on hers were strong but gentle, coaxing yet demanding, and she gave in willingly. The kiss was long and languid, and Rafe broke the embrace before she did.

"You aren't sex starved." His voice was a whisper in the quiet of the room.

She stared up into his gray eyes. Eyes that should have seemed cold were filled with heat—the heat of desire, and another deeper emotion that seemed out of step with the coldhearted man Rafe Santini thought himself to be.

"Are you?"

She had the insane desire to argue with him. True she wasn't sex starved, not now, after that wonderful lovemaking she'd shared with him. In his voice were no doubts, only the surety of a man who knew he'd loved his woman well.

"Cassie, do we need to do something more about your love-starved state?"

"No." The words were said jokingly as if he didn't believe she'd ever been in that state, but she had been. She'd never really been a passionate woman, and Rafe had made her realize all that she'd missed. Not that she was really sex starved, but she had been touch starved, love starved. She'd needed something more than Andy could fulfill. Something more than Rafe would be comfortable giving, something she was sure he didn't know he'd added to her soul. "I was not sex starved just...I don't know, something was missing."

"Me, too," he said after a moment. He rolled off her. He threw his arm up over his head, staring at the curtained canopy.

"Do you miss being close to one person?" she asked.

He sighed, a lost and lonely sound. "No."

Cass leaned up on her elbow, carefully tucking the sheet across her breasts. "What do you miss?"

"I miss being part of a family, speaking Italian and eating too much on holidays. I miss laughter."

Be a part of my family, Cass thought. I'll show you how to laugh again. But she couldn't say that out loud. Here in the dimly lit bedroom Rafe had revealed more of himself than he'd ever shown her before. She had more questions but didn't want him to clam up again. She bit her lip to keep from asking one of them now.

Cass wondered how it would feel to lose both parents suddenly. She wondered if she wouldn't become more like Rafe, afraid to chance loving someone.

"Rafe," she said, thinking to offer him some sort of comfort.

"Don't do it, Cassie. Don't think that I'm the missing link to your family and that you're the missing part of my life. I won't let myself be committed to *anyone*."

She fell to her back, not wanting him to see the emotions on her face. She gambled everything on last night, but the sharp pain around her heart told her that she'd made a huge judgment error. What was she going to do now? She fought to keep from crying for the second time that night. She'd stopped feeling awkward only to have him remind her there was nothing between them outside of this bed. Pride gave her the strength to say, "I didn't ask you to be a part of my family."

"Yes, you did." He shifted on the bed, looking down on her again. "And you deserve more than what a burned-out, coldhearted man like me can give you. I knew that before I took you to bed, and so did you."

"I'm not expecting a marriage proposal, Rafe Santini." He was right; she'd known that he wanted no commitment. But hearing him say the words out loud hurt. She pushed herself off the bed and searched the darkened bedroom for her dress.

She slipped it on and zipped it quickly. It hurt that Rafe didn't say a word as she left, but she hadn't really expected him to. She gathered her hose and purse, leaving behind the boxes of contraceptives. He'd use them before she did.

She walked out of the quiet room feeling as if her heart was breaking in two and knew that the damage might never be repaired, because Rafe would never let himself love her.

"Cassie, dammit, get back here." Rafe hopped from one foot to the other pulling on his cutoffs. Rafe knew that if she left him tonight, he'd never see her again. She'd avoid him and ignore him until... "Cassandra Gambrel, I'm not kidding. Stop right there."

She paused, facing straight ahead and not looking back at him. Damn, he hated the way she did that. Stood there, hurting without acknowledging him. The tense set of her shoulders and the correctness of her bearing told him that calming her down wasn't going to be easy.

He really could be an oaf. He'd never given a second thought to analyzing his feelings, and he believed in speaking his mind. But, hell, he'd never meant to hurt Cass. He realized now that he'd given her false hope.

He strode to her and wrapped his arms around her, pulling her back against his chest. He heard her uneven breathing and then felt her hot tears on his arm. Maybe keeping her here with him wasn't a good idea.

"Rafe," she said, her voice breaking on a sob. "Please don't touch me."

Stung, he released her and stepped back. He'd hurt her worse than he'd ever envisioned. "I'm sorry. I should have..."

She spun around to face him. Her gingery eyes bright with unshed tears. "It's not all your fault, Rafe. I knew what I was doing. And I resent the fact that you think I was coerced into making love with you."

Rafe should have backed away then, because he knew he was leaving himself wide open for trouble. But Cass had his attention now. And the thought of her leaving left him feeling angry and tense, and dammit it all, she was his woman whether she wanted to admit it or not. "Ah, hell, Cass. I know that."

"Then why do you insist on talking about this... relationship? Is that what we have Rafe?"

"I don't know what to call it," he said. And honestly he didn't. Matters had gone way beyond anything he'd experienced in past years, and he didn't know where they were leading.

"I don't know, either. The thought of having an affair makes me uncomfortable, but even worse is the concept of being a one-night stand. Is that all this is? Is that what you were trying to tell me when I left your bedroom?"

"It's not just a one-night stand." He reached out and caught her shoulder, tugging her back against his chest. "I don't know what to call this budding relationship of ours. I'm trying to be honest here. I'm no prize, Cass. I don't know why you haven't figured that out yet. You deserve better than me."

"Oh, Rafe. You're too hard on yourself."

"And you're too forgiving." He held her tight, even when she tried to turn in his embrace. "Stay still. I know that I'm not a good influence on Andy, or on you, for that matter. But dammit, woman, you're not walking out of here now."

He lifted her in his arms, cradling her to his chest. He carried her back to his bedroom and that big antique bed that was more Cass's than his.

In the back of his mind Rafe knew that this wasn't the ending, or a solution to the bigger problems they both faced, but right now it was what they both needed.

# Eleven

She'd lain awake until near dawn, anxiety plaguing her thoughts. She'd decided to enjoy her time with Rafe to the fullest. Like Scarlett, she'd think about her problems tomorrow. For now she'd take one day at a time and treasure each one.

She didn't have to pick up Andy until tomorrow after school, and she intended to enjoy the temporary freedom. She glanced at the clock and was surprised to see it was eleven. She felt like a slugabed as she snuggled deeper into Rafe's warmth.

She could get used to this so easily, but cautioned herself not to. Live for the moment, she thought. Despite her new determination, deep down she still hoped that she'd be able to convince Rafe they deserved a lifetime of happiness together. Cass believed that Rafe wouldn't be happy with less than a full-fledged commitment. She just had to convince him of that.

A shaft of sunlight pierced through the sheer curtains that

hung to the floor. The enclosed bed made her feel like she was sequestered on a faraway island. Her heart beat in synchronization with Rafe's, making her aware of the close proximity of their bodies. She listened to the mingled sound of their breathing and stared out the curtains.

Discarded clothing littered the floor like debris after a storm. Remembering the blazing desire that had flared out of control between her and Rafe made her blush. Passion had changed her into a woman she hardly recognized.

The sight of their intermingled clothing made her heart rejoice. She'd shared more with this man than with any other. She and Carl had never experienced the kind of burning passion that had ignited between her and Rafe.

His body cradled hers like a sexy teddy, barely covering her, but exciting her at the same time. His even breathing told her that he still slept. She snuggled closer to Rafe and froze when she felt his erection pressing into her.

She scooted a few inches away from him, but immediately missed his warmth. A quick look confirmed that Rafe was still asleep. Good, she didn't want to face him this morning, not while her blood was pumping to beat the band.

Rafe mumbled something in his sleep. He stretched and the sheet dipped low on his flat, washboard stomach. The light covering of hair on his chest tapered downward, and Cass wanted to trace the line. She reached out to him before realizing what she was doing.

Cass sat stunned. She'd never been the aggressor. Sex scared her on some level, and she'd been afraid to reach out to any man.

Rafe had changed all of that. She didn't want to be the subject of his desire, but an equal participant in it. She pulled her hand back, letting it drift down to lie next to his almost bare body on the bed. A few inches of pristine white sheet were all that saved his modesty.

Ha, she thought. Rafe didn't have a modest bone in his body. But she did. She thought briefly of tugging the sheet

up to cover his body, but knew he'd tease her if he woke
while she was doing that.

She bit her lip as she stared down at him. He was a fine
specimen of the male species. Something primitive and un-
tamed burst into life deep inside her. Rafe was a man who
would have been better suited to life in prehistoric times.
He was the all-conquering male. More warrior than civi-
lized gentleman. With a sort of stunned amazement, Cass
acknowledged she wouldn't have him any other way.

Gazing at the wide expanse of his chest, she remembered
the feel of his body on top of hers. The heat of his skin,
the texture of his hair, the raw power in him. She ran her
index finger along the line between his body and the bed.

She was glad that Rafe took pride in the way he looked.
Cass sighed. If she didn't get out of bed now she never
would. Sorting through the covers at the bottom of the bed,
she reached for a faded afghan. She wasn't going to pull
that sheet off him.

Standing, she tried to separate the afghan and the top
sheet, but her careful planning failed, and the remaining
sheet fell away. A ray of light shone brightly through the
bed curtains, bathing Rafe's nude body in the light. Cass
held her breath as she stared at him. The body that she'd
loved so well the night before looked different in full light.
This was the body that had made hers feel as if she were
soaring to the stars, the body that was the man she loved.

He sure was magnificently built. She sat perched on the
edge of the mattress, staring at him. Weak woman that she
was, she wanted to throw herself on top of him and love
him again. Tempt him to love her—really love her with his
heart and soul, using the only weapon he'd given her. But
she wouldn't. That would be dishonest, and as much as she
wanted Rafe permanently in her life, she wouldn't stoop to
using sex.

She wrapped the sheet around her torso and began sorting through the clothing on the floor. The bed springs
creaked, and she glanced at the bed. Rafe's dark form made

an imposing shadow behind the sheer drapes. He moved restlessly, rolling onto his stomach.

She bent and retrieved the first item of clothing available. Rafe's shirt. It was one of the ones she'd given him, and she knew he liked it because she'd seen him wearing it several times.

She held the shirt to her face for a moment, inhaling the scent of Rafe. He was essential male and his scent enhanced that quality. She slid her arms into the sleeves and let the sheet fall away.

She fastened the front, trying to convince herself that she hadn't picked up his shirt because she'd wanted to feel embraced by him. Unable to help herself, she wandered back to the bed and stared through the sheer drapes at him. Rafe's backside was clearly visible. Cute buns, she thought with a grin.

Her fingers tingled with the need to touch him. She reached through the panels and lightly caressed his back. The skin was warm, hard, tempting… She raked her nails down the length of him, following his spine to the firm flesh of his buttocks.

He shivered and moved under her touch. She opened her palm and rubbed her hand down over his buttocks before moving on to his legs. She stopped at his feet and knew she couldn't continue. The man was sleeping, for pity's sake. She removed her hand, pulling the sheet up over him with a quick flick of her wrist.

Cass had never thought of herself as sex crazed, but she was certainly beginning to feel that way. She had never felt this restless yearning, this needing to bond with someone else, this…love.

She left his bedroom as if the hounds of hell were chasing her. She went to the kitchen, gulping in deep draughts of air. Oh, heaven, help her. She was only just realizing the pain that Rafe could inflict upon her. If he left her, he'd take her soul with him.

* * *

Rafe knew exactly what he wanted from life. At this moment he wanted—no needed—a certain shy lady who had left him in an uncomfortable position. He'd almost rolled over and pulled her back into bed when he'd felt her soft fingers against his back, but instinct had stayed the motion. Cass was bound to feel awkward this morning, and he was feeling gentlemanly.

The sun painted shadows on the wall, and Rafe closed his eyes against them. For the first time in years he felt almost at peace with his life, and that scared the hell out of him. Cass had wrought changes in him that she didn't even know about. Since making love to her last night he'd felt different.

He stretched and yawned before standing up and donning a pair of faded denim cutoffs. He fastened the snap, then paused as the sound of returning footsteps reached him. Briefly he debated hopping back into bed and seeing if she'd rejoin him.

His breath caught in his chest as she re-entered the room. She looked so sweet, so tender—and so capable of breaking his heart. Her hair hung in disarray around her shoulders, the curly length of it beckoning him to try to tame it. His shirt hugged her curves in a way that made his cutoffs uncomfortable. She smiled that shy half smile of hers, and Rafe groaned out loud.

He knew then that he should back away. Physically she wasn't ready for him, not right now. And emotionally he wasn't ready for her; he might never be. The silence lengthened, and he cleared his throat, hoping to catch her attention. "I started the coffee," she said.

Her voice, still husky with sleep, brushed over his already aroused senses like a match to kindling. She stared at a point somewhere over his left shoulder. He wondered if she'd ever look him in the eye again. A faint blush covered her face, and he knew she was remembering her earlier boldness. He hated that she felt embarrassed by something natural.

He opened his arms, and she walked right into them. Her slender frame fit perfectly against his. Just remembering the rightness of their embrace last night added fuel to an already burning fire.

"Cassie, baby, you're making me crazy. Why did you leave my bed this morning?" he asked, then cradled her until she settled in his arms, her head resting over his heart.

"You were awake?" Her soft voice had changed to a croak. She pressed her face into his chest, and he knew she was blushing.

Cass refused to look up at him, so he lifted her chin with his hand. "Why didn't you stay?"

She shook her head, refusing to answer. Rafe hugged her and bent to taste her. Last night seemed like a distant memory, and his soul clamored for more of her. Her lips parted beneath his without any coaxing, and she leaned up into him. Her arms wrapped around his neck, and her body brushed against his chest and groin.

His hands twisted in her hair as he tried to meld deeper into her mouth. His grasp ran the length of her back, and he cupped the pert cheeks of her buttocks. Damn, the woman felt good in his arms. The womanly heat of her burned him through the thin layer of her clothing.

He let his fingers tease up under the shirt and was surprised to find she was naked. He groaned again, the sound almost animal—feral in hunger. He thrust one thigh between her legs and felt her moist heat.

He left her mouth to taste the sensitive skin on her neck. She gasped as he nibbled his way down…down to the collar of her shirt and lower still to the tempting bounty beyond.

Her full breasts greeted him eagerly, aching to have their need fulfilled. He suckled her flesh through the cotton of the shirt, her hard nipple pouting up at him. He pulled back and blew gently on the aroused flesh.

Cass moaned, a sound drawn from the back of her throat. She held him closer with her hands and offered her body to him. She twisted against him with all her strength, pulling his mouth back to her breasts when he didn't respond immediately to her coaxing.

Rafe returned to do her bidding and almost lost his balance when she bucked against him. Cass was teetering on the precipice of completion.

Rafe felt like he would burst if he didn't get inside of her soon, didn't feel her soft body comforting, closing, caressing his into climax. He started for the bed, the most basic need to mate with Cass driving him. He shouldered his way past the curtains. Cass's soft gasp as he practically threw her onto the bed brought Rafe to his senses.

Dammit, man, slow down, he cautioned himself. But knew the out-of-control effect she had on him wreaked havoc with his plans. "Ah, baby. I'm sorry."

"Rafe," she said, her voice once again caressing him. "Hurry up."

If she'd said that at any other moment he'd have laughed out loud, but he was dangerously close to the edge. He unfastened his cutoffs and kicked them aside before reaching for the box of contraceptives that still sat on the nightstand.

By the time he'd sheathed himself in a condom, Cass had discarded her shirt. She lay back on the pillows, her arms opened to him, and Rafe knew he was in love with her. He couldn't wait a moment longer to join her on the bed.

He covered her, and she reached up for him. Their mouths met and tongues dueled, and Rafe reached down to test her readiness. Cass's warmth spilled onto his hand, and he used it to lubricate his entrance into her tight sheath.

It was like being wrapped in fire; hot, pulsing fire that brought him closer to heaven. He groaned and thrust harder. Cass rose to meet his hips with each thrust, and he felt the tingles of his completion along the edge of his spine.

He reached between their bodies and coaxed Cass over the edge first, then emptied himself into her waiting body

with a force he'd never experienced before. His breathing
was heavy and labored, and he cuddled her close before
rolling to his back.

"Ah, hell, Cassie."

She sighed and reached up to push his hair off his forehead. "Don't cuss."

He laughed and hugged her closer. No other woman had
ever touched his soul the way she did. She was a comfort
to him, filling those empty black spaces with light.

Rafe settled deeply into the bed and held Cass firmly by
his side. Sleep beckoned like a mother comforting a scared
child, and Rafe felt himself drifting slowly toward…

"Is it Gicalone?" Cass asked.

"What?" Rafe stared down into her beautiful gingery
eyes and forgot what she'd asked.

"You're middle name?"

"No. It's Gen—" He bent and bit her lightly on her
neck. "Tricky, Ms. Gambrel, but I'm not going to reveal
that name."

She just laughed, and Rafe groaned, knowing the chance
for sleep was gone. But he didn't mind. Something inside
of him said to enjoy every moment with her while it lasted.

Cass stared out the window and watched the rain drift
slowly down the glass pane. Rafe had suggested they return
to her house after they'd eaten lunch in case Andy needed
them. The gesture touched her more than it should have.

The cool, wet weather made it feel almost like Christmas.
The first tingles of holiday excitement shivered through her.
She wanted to share her enthusiasm for the season with
Rafe, but doubted he'd be thrilled at the thought of another
holiday alone.

But he wouldn't be alone this year, Cass vowed. She and
Andy would bring him into the protective fold of their family. Whether he wanted to be there or not.

She missed Andy, but didn't want to rock the boat with
Rafe. The afternoon had been wonderful. Rafe had the po-

tential to be a wonderful life mate. But he felt differently, and he'd been frank about not wanting to be a substitute daddy to her son.

*Don't think that I'm the missing link to your family.* She sighed and forced herself to think about the coming week. She had to start hanging her Christmas decorations and buy a tree.

Rafe walked up behind her and wrapped his arms around her. She leaned against him and felt at home. She started to sigh again, but forced herself to stop. She was beginning to feel like a melodramatic heroine from a grade-B movie. "I'll have to buy a tree sometime this week."

"Do you want to go now and look for one?"

His casual offer meant more to Cass than any dozen roses ever would. "Are you sure?"

Rafe exhaled a bit unsteadily, but didn't answer. He dropped a kiss on the top of her head before pulling away from her. "Go get a jacket."

"We'd have to pick up Andy first."

He gave her an aggrieved look. "I know."

She shrugged and forced herself not to smile. Rafe thought he was concealing his motives, but she could read him like a book. She knew that her son had grown fond of their neighbor over the past few weeks, but had no idea that Rafe reciprocated the feeling to this extent.

"Okay," she said. "Want to take my car?"

She hoped that by acting as if nothing out of the ordinary had occurred, he would, too. She crossed to the hall closet and grabbed her faded denim jacket.

"Okay. I'll drive."

"Why?" she asked as they headed out to her car.

"Because..." He glanced over at her.

"I'm waiting," she said. She just knew that he was going to make some stupid, macho remark about men being better drivers.

"I prefer to drive," he said diplomatically. He held her door open, something he'd never done before.

"Don't think that one chivalrous gesture is going to make up for your behavior."

"Honey, I told you I was no gentleman," he warned before closing the door.

Cass watched him walk around to the driver's side and silently disagreed with him. Rafe's code of honor made him more of a gentleman than any other man she knew.

"You don't mind picking up Andy?" she asked when they were on their way.

"No, Cass, I don't."

Cass realized then that Rafe had missed her son as much as she had. She also knew that he was trying to find a way to keep the peace between them. So she stifled the remaining questions she had. Her relationship with Rafe was as fragile as spun glass, but Cass could see it growing stronger by the hour. Already Rafe was wanting to involve himself in her life.

Andy came running out of her mother's house as they pulled up. Cass felt a tug on her heartstrings as her small son hurled himself into her arms. "Mom, I missed you."

"I missed you, too, honey." She dropped a quick kiss on his head.

He quickly pulled free and glanced over at Rafe, then looked up at her with one of those questioning looks of his. He wanted to know if it was okay to hug Rafe. She honestly didn't know if Rafe would rebuff her son. She shook her head after a moment, not wanting to put Rafe's newfound eagerness to be a part of their family to the test.

"Hi, Mr. Santini," Andy said.

"Hi, pal."

Something close to disappointment shone on Rafe's face and Cass wondered if he would have welcomed Andy's hug.

"Why did you come, Mr. Santini?" Andy asked.

"I decided it was time to shop for a Christmas tree."

"All right," he shouted. "I'll be ready to go in a minute."

Cass watched Andy sprint into the house. Rafe came up behind her and wrapped his arm around her shoulder. They followed her son into the house.

Cass had the feeling that something inside of Rafe had changed. Something hard and unfeeling. Something that he'd kept hidden all these years.

# Twelve

The tree lot was filled with Christmas noises and happy people. Sounds and sights that Rafe generally ignored, he found appealing today. Carols blared loudly from mounted speakers, and Andy grabbed his hand as they walked through the lot.

Andy's small hand, clasped in his, felt right. Rafe didn't feel the urge to pull away from the kid's obvious affection the way he usually did.

"Here's the one I want," Andy said.

The boy had been talking a mile a minute since they'd picked him up. Rafe refused to puzzle over the odd disappointment he'd felt when Andy had greeted his mother with a hug and not him. Some things, he'd learned, were better left unexplored.

He forced his attention to the tree Andy pointed out. Rafe bit back a groan. Even Charlie Brown had better taste than the kid. The large, scrawny tree that Andy wanted to buy was... Rafe wanted to be supportive of the boy's decision, remembering himself at that age, but what the hell was he supposed to say?

"What do you think, Cass?" he asked.

"No, that one's too...large."

He glanced at her, and she shrugged. The tree *was* tall, Rafe conceded. He noticed that Cass was still staring at him.

"It'll touch the ceiling." He hoped that was what she'd been wanting him to say. He didn't know how to handle these father-type things. He thrust his hands into his jeans pockets.

Andy danced back and forth from one foot the other. "Oh, Mom. We can cut it down."

How Cass resisted the plea in her son's face, Rafe didn't understand. If he were Andy's father, the boy would be so impossibly spoiled it wouldn't be funny. Rafe realized fatherhood was more complex than he'd ever imagined.

Cass wrapped her arm around her small son's shoulders. "No, we can't. Remember last year's tree?"

Mother and son started laughing. The obvious love between them made Rafe uncomfortable. Yet at the same time, the sound touched a hidden place in his soul. It was one of the happiest Rafe had heard in a long time. It also left him feeling isolated and on the outside. He reminded himself that he was happy with his life.

"I'll help trim it," he volunteered, hating to see the light of excitement extinguished in the little boy's eyes.

"You won't have to. I've found another tree," Cass said. "Follow me."

Rafe watched Cass walk down the path, her hips swaying gently with each step she took. The khaki pants she wore were baggy, yet as she bent over to examine the trunk of the tree, they pulled tightly across her backside. Rafe's hands tingled with the need to touch those curves again.

"Here it is," she said, glancing up at him with excitement in her eyes. "This is the perfect tree."

She maneuvered a medium-sized pine tree out into the

aisle. Rafe stared at Cass. The bright bulbs of the Christmas tree lot highlighted her thick, curly hair, and joy shone from her eyes. He knew then that this Christmas memory would remain with him forever.

Her selection was flawless. The height and breadth would fill the living room without overpowering it. They discussed its merits, Rafe not quite believing that he was here, picking out a tree for the holiday. Damn, if he didn't feel good.

"All right, Mom," Andy said, slowly circling the tree.

He joined his mother at the tree and their words faded to Rafe. All he could envision were past Christmases when he'd gone hunting for the perfect tree with his dad. That had always been the man's job in his family.

He could almost smell his dad's pipe and hear his heavily accented English asking for the price on the tree. He remembered his father arguing with the lot owner and bargaining for a better price. He remembered the joy he'd felt at being included in the choice of the tree.

"Rafe?" Cass asked.

"Yeah?"

"Do you like this one?"

Her upturned face with eyes so trusting and full of life tore at him. He wanted to wrap her in his arms and cherish her for all his days. He wanted to make sure that she had everything she ever needed and that her son would have a father as he grew up.

"It's wonderful. I've never seen a better Christmas tree, except for the one Andy picked out."

"It's okay, Rafe. Mom's tree is better."

"Let's go pay for the tree," Andy suggested, taking Rafe's hand once more. "Mom, you guard the tree."

Rafe chuckled. For someone so small in stature, Andy could be a bulldozer when he wanted to. They reached the lot owner, and Rafe felt his dad's spirit with him once more as he haggled with the man over the price of the tree. Andy scampered away to tell Cass the tree was paid for.

"Nice-looking boy you have there," the lot owner said.

Rafe's first impulse was to correct the man, to tell him that the boy wasn't his son. But the man's words sounded right to his ears. He watched Andy disappear around the corner to where Cass was waiting, before turning back to the man. "Yes, he is."

When he returned to the tree, Cass glanced up at him and ventured a small smile. Rafe smiled back and reached out to ruffle Andy's hair. Rafe carried the tree to the Volvo. Andy handed him a bungee cord, and together they finished securing the tree.

"Okay, guys. Let's head home, and I'll fix you some hot chocolate," Cass said.

Rafe drove home, marveling over the changes in himself that had occurred while he was in the tree lot. He liked the thought of being Andy's father, and that scared him. He joined in the Christmas carol Andy and Cass were singing. He wanted no outside worries to intrude on the joy of this day.

Rafe's light mood was contagious. He teased, laughed and sang along with the Christmas songs on the radio. His valiant effort at enjoying the day wasn't lost on her. She hoped that their relationship would take a smooth, even keel after this, but didn't delude herself.

She knew Rafe hated the holidays, knew that they were painful and reminded him of all he'd lost. But she'd hoped this year would be different for him, that somehow she could show him how to love again.

Cass started opening boxes, searching for her tree lights. She found them in a tangled heap at the bottom of the last box she opened. "Here they are."

Rafe stared at the electrician's nightmare she was holding, and grimaced. "What the hell happened to them?"

"Rafe!" she said, hoping he'd learn to stop cussing.

"Cass!" he mimicked back. "Hand the lights over and I'll try to fix them."

"Mom's not very handy," Andy offered.

"No, she's not." Rafe smiled at her, and Cass grinned back. Remembering the day she'd helped him on his roof, she could well imagine what Rafe thought of her handiness.

"But you shouldn't cuss at her."

Cass bit the inside of her cheek to keep from laughing. Rafe took the reprimand in stride, reaching down to ruffle Andy's hair. "You're right, son. I apologize, Cass."

An apology from Rafe Santini. Cass couldn't keep the smile off her face this time, and the look on Rafe's face promised retribution. Cass winked at him to show him she wasn't afraid. "I'll go check on the cookies while you two fix the lights."

"A woman's place is in the kitchen."

She heard Rafe's comment as soon as she stepped out of the living room. She knew he'd meant it to rile her, but she ignored it. She'd retaliate later, she thought, when they were alone.

She knew that things weren't smoothed out between her and Rafe. She didn't lie to herself and pretend that he would want to marry her, now or ever. But she was glad to see him starting to show an interest in the holidays, and in her family.

He'd changed from the sullen man who'd planned to spend Thanksgiving Day in a bar. She hoped that she'd helped him, but couldn't help wondering if it wasn't time healing the wound. She sighed and took another lump of dough from the refrigerator.

She rolled out the batter and placed the cookies on the tray. Suddenly she had the feeling she was being watched. She glanced over her shoulder and found Rafe lounging in the doorway. He propped one shoulder casually against the door and tried to look tame.

Something about his expression reminded her of the first morning they'd met. He'd stood in her sunny kitchen looking out of place and read her the riot act for letting her son knock on a stranger's door. She now set the rolling pin aside and pivoted to face him.

"Where's Andy?" she asked.

"I asked him to let Tundra out into my backyard. Do you mind?"

"No, why would I?" She watched Rafe carefully, wondering what he was thinking. It was clear to her that he didn't like the new way he was acting toward her family, but he seemed unable to help himself.

"I don't know. Ah, hell, Cass, you shouldn't leave your son alone with me. You don't know what kind of influence I might be on him. I cuss all the time."

"Did you curse at him?" Cass asked, walking closer to him.

"No, of course not. But you know how I am."

That he was concerned about his language reassured her more than any other thing in the world could have. "I'm sure it'll be okay. Andy knows that I'll punish him if he uses bad words."

"You'd punish him for something that I taught him?" Rafe asked, sounding incredulous.

"Rafe, it's not like I spank him. He can't have dessert if he uses those words."

"You're kidding?"

"Well, I sometimes use some words that I shouldn't, so we had to have a punishment that could be meted out to either one of us. I don't pay him an allowance, so a 'swear jar' was out of the question."

"Good idea, Cass."

"Thanks. Come sit down and have some cookies."

"I'd better not. I'll try to follow your rules while I'm in your house, okay?"

"Sure, but why don't you want any cookies?"

"I've been using *bad words* since I was fourteen."

She smiled in understanding. "Oh, Rafe..."

"Stop giving me that look," he said in a disgruntled tone. He pulled her into his arms, engulfing her in a bear hug.

"What look?" Cass tilted her head back and gazed into

his brilliant gray eyes. His glance dropped to her lips, and Cass realized how warm and sexy he felt, pressed against her in the fragrant kitchen.

"The one that makes me want to pull you onto my lap and kiss you senseless."

"Oh." She licked her lips, hoping to entice him into kissing her. He leaned closer, his breath brushing across her mouth. Cass stood on her toes so that merely a space of daylight separated their mouths.

"Rafe," she said, dying for him to kiss her.

"What?"

Annoying man, she thought. She took the initiative from him and planted her lips on his. His mouth opened under hers immediately, and she thrust her tongue into the cavern of his mouth. He returned her advances, move for move, until Cass's blood tingled in her veins. She ran her hands across his shoulders to his neck and up into his thick hair.

The front door slammed shut, and Cass jerked away from Rafe. She wrapped her arms around her waist and took several deep breaths before glancing at Rafe.

"Hell," he said softly, running his hand through his hair. "Woman, you're a bundle of temptation."

The twinkle in his eye teased her into forgetting about their embrace. "You shouldn't have ventured into my domain."

Rafe quirked an eyebrow at her. "I'll give. Why?"

"Stay out of the kitchen if you can't stand the heat."

Rafe laughed so hard he doubled over. Cass enjoyed amusing Rafe and joking with him. She felt as if she'd given him a gift. She smiled to herself.

Andy came into the kitchen and dived for the cookies cooling on the counter. "Wash your hands, Andy," she said automatically.

"Oh, Mom."

"Oh, son," she replied.

Andy quickly washed his hands and bounded back into the room. "What's for dinner?"

Cass groaned. The thought of fixing dinner on top of all the baking she'd done this afternoon.

"How's pizza sound?" Rafe asked.

"Great!" Andy said.

"Let's go out," Rafe suggested.

Cass agreed. They needed to get away from the house. She didn't trust herself alone with Rafe. Lord help her, but that man set her blood to boiling.

The night air was cooler now. Even Rafe wore a sweater against the chill as they sat on her front porch swing. She relaxed against his shoulder, loving the feel of him beside her. She had always imagined that this was the way married life would be, but Carl had been too busy to sit on the porch after Andy's birth.

Several houses in the neighborhood had decorated their yards for Christmas, and lighted Santas and reindeer cast a soft glow on the street. Rafe stroked her shoulder in a soothing way, and Cass felt at peace as she hadn't in years.

"Rafe, I need some advice."

"Shoot," he said. His fingers were working their way between her cardigan and her shirt. She felt the rasp of his callused palm on the cotton of her blouse. Her breasts started to tingle, longing for his touch.

"Stop that," she said, grabbing his wrist and pulling his hand to her lap. "I'm serious."

He sighed, an exaggerated sound that made her smile. "Okay, I'm listening."

"I've decided to let Andy start taking karate lessons in January. Actually, I'm giving him the lessons as a gift."

"And?" he asked.

Cass faced him on the swing. "I'm not sure this is the right decision. I mean he's never been involved in sports before and well, you mentioned martial arts and so I thought…"

Cass knew she was rambling, but she was unsure if she'd made the right decision. She needed someone to tell her she had, or at least help to understand why she hadn't. Sometimes she felt that she'd made the decision just to gain Rafe's approval.

"I don't know, Cass. I firmly believe that athletics help a young man, but I have no idea how it will affect Andy. Martial arts have a strong belief in discipline, and I guarantee that he'll listen to you when you tell him not to leave the house."

"But is it the right decision?"

He stared at her, his face drawn and tense a swirling mass of conflicting emotions arising in him. "Don't ask me, Cass. I'm not his father. I have zero experience at being a parent, and I can't help."

She stood and strode to the porch railing. Every discussion and argument they had seemed to come back to that one fact. "Rafe Santini, you make me so mad."

"I know." He walked up behind her, wrapping his arms around her. "I know, babe. But I don't want to give you the wrong advice. Honestly, I'm not qualified to offer you my opinion."

She relaxed against him. "Okay. I didn't mean to pressure you."

"Are we done talking?" he asked. He toyed with the hem of her sweater, and Cass knew what he was thinking. "Want to go inside."

"Yes," she said, trying to turn in his embrace, but he refused to let her. He unbuttoned the cardigan and pushed the sides out of his way. He caressed her sensitive skin through the light layer of her cotton shirt. "What about Andy?"

His thumb and forefinger plucked at her nipples, and they hardened under his touch. He kissed her neck, using his teeth and tongue to excite her. Cass wanted to rip her clothes off and throw herself at him.

"I guess we'll have to wait for another night," he said, sounding disappointed. He rebuttoned her sweater and led her back over to the front porch swing. Cass settled down beside him and let the rocking chair lull her toward sleep.

"I want to wear my naughty nightie for you," she said after a few minutes.

"Let's go away for the weekend," Rafe suggested.

"Oh, I'd love to." She imagined that going away with Rafe would be the most exciting thing that had happened to her in a long time. But in her heart of hearts she knew he would never learn to accept that she was bound to her family if she allowed him to treat her like a single lady.

"I'm sensing that you're not going to say yes."

She stared up at him in the dim light of the moon. He didn't look resigned or disappointed. It seemed he knew that she couldn't run away and leave her son with his grandmother all the time.

"I'll sweeten the pot," he said, kissing her gently on the brow. "We can take Andy with us and go over to Busch Gardens in Tampa."

"We could just stay home and enjoy the local sights."

"What local sights? Disney? EPCOT? You really want to fight those crowds?" he asked.

"I don't know. But I don't want to go away this close to Christmas. There are a million things I have to do."

"Okay, so we'll wait until after the holidays."

Cass agreed, and they let silence drift around them. They stayed that way until the cold forced them into the house. Rafe kissed her sweetly on her doorstep before going home.

Cass knew then what she was going to do. Before Christmas she was going to ask Rafe Santini to marry her.

# Thirteen

Rafe loved the feel of the crisp fall air on his face as he jogged through the housing development. Tundra ran ahead and fell behind him at intervals. For once he felt at peace with the world.

Rafe tried to ignore the questions rumbling in his head. Questions about his life and the new feelings of love that Cass generated in him. He'd been thinking of putting some distance between himself and Cass.

He'd tried to keep things light between them, but his instincts were hard to suppress. He craved family the way an alcoholic craved liquor. The double impact of having Christmas waiting around the corner wasn't helping. Every time he tried to pull back emotionally from Cass he remembered the loneliness of the past few years.

He reassured himself daily that he wasn't harming Cass and Andy, but he was waiting for the other shoe to drop. Expecting trouble around every corner. Past experience had taught him to beware of caring, that every time he allowed himself to open up to another person, he'd be hurt.

He slowed his pace as he rounded the corner and started down the home stretch. Without conscious thought, his gaze sought out Cass's house. Rafe cursed under his breath. The damn fool woman was standing on a ladder trying to hang her Christmas lights. Considering she had a two-story house, she was asking for trouble doing the job on her own. Why the hell didn't she ask him?

Cass made him crazy. The woman took chances that no sane person would. She seemed determined to complete every job by herself. He knew she'd been on her own for a long time, but it was time that she learned to ask for help.

Tundra announced their arrival, and Cass braced herself on the ladder before glancing down at him. She smiled, a brilliant explosion of joy that warmed his heart. Rafe forgot his aggravation with her as he watched her hips swaying with each step she took down the ladder.

Her jeans clung to her seat and Rafe wanted to reach out and caress her. He wanted to shape her flesh with his hands. Unable to help himself, he encircled her waist and pulled her back against his chest. She twisted her head around, and he claimed a kiss.

The physical side of their relationship suited Rafe to a T. He missed sleeping with her, but she always responded to his kisses and embraces with a generous passion that never failed to surprise him. It wasn't sex that he missed, but the holding, the comforting, the loving.

He held her loosely in his arms. "What are you doing?"

Her wide ginger-colored eyes met his as she shrugged.

He was amazed at the different levels this woman reached him on. She was the most passionate lover he'd ever had, but she was also the most caring, considerate person he'd ever met. In his mind those two identities should be separate.

His past affairs had been lustful liaisons. Brief, mean-ingless encounters with women, where the only thing they

had in common was the fever of desire. Not the fierce burning need he felt for Cass—more like an itch that needed
scratching. He couldn't even remember the names or the
faces of those women now. Somehow they'd all blended
into Cass.

She felt like the other half of his soul—the empty half
that he'd tried to bury. Somehow she'd sneaked past his
guard and forced him to care about her. Honesty compelled
him to admit to himself that Cass hadn't done any forcing.
He'd needed her to burrow inside his heart and remind him
of all that he'd tried to forget.

"Do you need some help with the lights?" he asked,
needing to keep his thoughts from dwelling on things like
how much she reminded him of home. Not the house he'd
grown up in, but the safe, well-loved feeling that his family
had given him.

He remembered his dad reading his mother the same lecture on learning to ask for help. He tried to recall the words,
but only one thought remained—his dad telling him that
women depended on men to protect them and cherish them.
*Never forget that, son.*

His father's words rang in his head, unsettling Rafe. The
similarities between his parents' relationship and his own
relationship with Cass didn't end there. He could endanger
her the way he'd hurt them.

A hard lump formed in his throat. He knew better than
to start caring. Hadn't he learned a valuable lesson with his
parents' death? His mother's superstitious nature had
rubbed off on Rafe, and he felt that his memory of his dad
was a warning. Back away now, he thought, before anyone
gets hurt.

Suddenly the day started closing in around him. He pan-
icked, though he would never admit it to another living
soul. The need to escape overwhelmed him.

Before she could answer his question her phone rang.
"Want to come inside?"

No, he thought, but he couldn't say that. As much as he wanted to escape, he knew he needed to stay. "Sure."

Rafe followed her into her inviting home. He always felt enveloped in the warmth of the place. Rafe started a pot of coffee while Cass took the phone call. He concentrated on remembering that he was a bachelor and set in his ways. He didn't want the pain or the responsibility that came along with being married. No matter how much a certain lady with ginger-colored eyes made him think otherwise.

He wanted to seek comfort from her, have her cradle him in her arms. He needed to bury the past memories and start again with new ones. But was the pain worth it?

Cass needed commitment. Ah, hell, she needed marriage. She needed a man who would help her make decisions about Andy's future. Damn, life was hard.

"Rafe?"

Her voice was husky with repressed emotion. Rafe set the coffee filters on the counter and crossed the room, gathering her in his arms. "What is it?"

"Andy was in another fight."

"Another one?"

"Yes, he's been having problems adjusting to his new class."

She rubbed her forehead with her fingers. The tension, worry and frustration in her was clearly evident. "I've got to go pick him up. He's been suspended from school."

Cass stepped away from him, and Rafe shut off the coffeepot before following her out into the hall. All his earlier thoughts of escape fled. He couldn't leave her alone now. She needed him. She was coming back down the stairs when he opened the hall closet.

"Why is Andy suspended?" Rafe asked, holding a jacket out for her.

"He started the fight."

Rafe trailed behind Cass, unsure of what to do. Should he offer to go with her? Did he really want to? She couldn't drive herself, he argued. Not in the shape she was in. "I'll drive down with you."

For a moment gratitude shone from her eyes. She started to hand him her keys, but then seemed to remember their agreement—casual involvement—nothing serious.

"It's okay," he said, taking the keys. "I want to go with you."

"Thanks," she said, hurrying around to the passenger side and climbing into the car.

Cass sat tensely, staring out the window. He tried several times to start a conversation with her, but nothing worked. He figured she was worried about Andy being hurt and tried to reassure her. "Cass, I'm sure Andy's fine."

"How can you be sure?" she asked, her tone sassy.

"I've been teaching him self-defense."

Cass was silent for so long that Rafe began doubting his actions. He should have asked her first. It didn't matter that Andy had assured him that Cass wouldn't mind.

"I just showed him a few basic moves. Nothing that could hurt another person. The moves are mainly used for self-defense."

"Where was I?" she asked.

"In town picking up that ottoman at Mrs. Feuller's."

"Was he a good student, Rafe?"

"Yes."

Silence deepened between them, and Rafe called himself every name in the book. If he hadn't shown those moves to Andy, the boy probably would have walked away from the confrontation that now had him sitting in the principal's office.

"You mentioned signing him up for karate, so I thought I'd show him a few moves and see if he liked it, before you wasted your money." Somehow, all his reasons and explanations sounded lame now. Sure, he hadn't meant for Andy to start a fight, but he hadn't known how the boy would use the knowledge, either.

She nodded, but still only stared at him, not saying a

word. She had that look on her face as if she was about to
cry. Rafe reiterated a few of the choice names he'd just
called himself.

He pulled to a stop in front of the administration building
at the elementary school. He reached for the door handle,
needing to escape the confines of the car and his own
thoughts. But Cass's fingers on his sleeve stopped him.

He glanced over at her, and she started crying. "Thank
you, Rafe. I know that involvement with my son is the one
thing you've been trying to avoid, but it means a lot to me
that you taught him how to defend himself."

She leaned over and kissed him lightly on the lips. He
wiped the tear tracks from her face and brushed her bangs
off her forehead. Rafe knew he was doomed. "Want me to
come in with you?"

"Please," she said. "I hope I don't embarrass Andy by
crying all over him."

Rafe came around the car, and together they walked into
the school building. "I'm sure he'll understand your tears,
honey."

Cass smiled up at him with gratitude, and Rafe hoped
that he'd never see hurt or disappointment in her eyes
again. He took a deep breath and followed Cass through
the double door, remembering his first experience in the
principal's office.

Andy sat in the backseat of the Volvo, staring out the
window. Cass refused to give in to the need to sweep Andy
into her arms and squeeze the stuffing out of him. A big
part of her wanted to cuddle her son in her arms, but she
knew that he'd never learn a lesson if she treated him like
a baby.

The sullen, moody way he was acting reminded her that
he'd be a teenager one day. She sighed and looked over at
Rafe. He shrugged as if to say he didn't know what to do,
either.

Cass was at her wits' end. She couldn't get through to

Andy and had no idea how to break down the walls he was putting up.

Glancing over her shoulder, she bit her lip over Andy's scrapes. His face looked horrid. His right eye was swelling, and his upper lip had blood dried on it. She wanted to hug him to her side and never let him leave the house again. Cass pulled a package of Wet Ones from the glove box and handed them to Andy.

He quietly wiped at his lip, trying to remove the dried blood. Cass reached out and took the wet tissue from him and finished cleaning the area. Rafe stopped the car at a light.

"Andy, did you start that fight?" Cass asked quietly.

He stared at his lap for a few seconds, then glanced out the window again.

"Answer your mother, Andy."

Rafe surprised Cass by getting involved. At the school he'd been quiet and supportive but hadn't said a word.

"Not exactly."

"Tell me *exactly* what happened." Cass tried to stay calm, warned herself not to lose it. But the thought of her son in a fight...

"Jeff called me a skinny geek. I called him an overweight oaf. He punched me, I punched him back."

Andy, the king of understatement. "You know how I feel about fighting—"

"Ah, hell, Mom. This time I at least knew how to stand up for myself. Last time he just beat me to a pulp, and everyone stared at me."

"Don't cuss," she said softly. Cass understood now that Andy needed to be able to defend himself or he'd never develop into a man. Rafe had given her a greater gift than she'd realized.

"Okay, I can understand that. But from now on, try to walk away first."

"I'll try."

Rafe pulled into the driveway, shutting off the engine.

Silence descended, and no one made a move to get out of the car. Cass finally ordered Andy up to his room. He had three days worth of assignments to complete.

"Rafe?" Andy asked, standing at the front door.

"Yeah, pal?"

"Thanks," he said, before running into the house and slamming the door behind him.

Rafe shook his head. Cass smiled to herself, enjoying the moment.

"I'm going home to wash up. Want to go out for dinner tonight?"

"I'll see if I can get a sitter."

"Andy can come with us."

"No, he can't. He has to stay home and remember that fighting is wrong."

Rafe looked like he wanted to object, but he didn't say anything else. He started walking across the street to his house. "Call me later."

"Rafe?" He glanced back at her. "Thanks again."

He nodded and continued across the street. It occurred to Cass that Rafe wasn't comfortable with the role he'd played in this afternoon's fiasco, but she was buoyed by the fact that he'd played any role at all.

More than anything she wanted to savor Rafe's new attitude toward her. She wanted to relive the way he'd looked at her when she'd asked him to go into the school with her.

Tonight was the night, she thought. Rafe's new attitude made her think he'd welcome a talk about a deeper relationship. She went inside the house, planning the evening in her head.

Cass called Rafe and invited him over for dinner, before driving Andy over to Jeff Lowell's house. Jeff's mom, Dana, was a personal friend of Cass's, and both women agreed that the boys needed to spend time together. Dana offered to take the boys for the night, and Cass was going to watch them tomorrow while Dana was at work.

Cass hurried home, stopping at the market for a bottle of champagne. She changed into her tempting red nightgown and lit candles throughout the downstairs area. In the living room she put her favorite Harry Connick, Jr., CD on.

The doorbell rang, and Cass paused in front of the hall mirror to look at herself. Suddenly she had a few doubts about answering the door in this getup. What if it was a neighbor wanting to borrow something? She grabbed a jacket before heading to the door.

"Who is it?"

"It's me, baby."

Rafe's voice poured over her like honey on a warm day. Her pulse tripped over itself as her heart started to beat quicker. She opened the door and felt desire rush through her, pooling at her center.

Rafe wore a pair of tight jeans and one of the shirts she'd given him, an aqua-colored T-shirt that molded to the muscles of his chest. She tried to smile, but all she could do was stare at his face. Not handsome in a California-Hollywood way, but attractive because of the character shown there. The rugged look of a man who lived life to the fullest.

"Cassie?" He stepped over the threshold.

"Sorry," she muttered and turned to replace her jacket in the closet. She used that moment to try to regain her control. To remind herself that she wasn't going to jump his bones.

A low wolf whistle sounded, and she pivoted to face him. "Hell, Cassie, you're so damn sexy."

"It's the negligee."

"No," he said, firmly. The heat of desire in his eyes made shivers course down her spine. "It's you."

She flushed at the compliment and led the way into the living room where she'd set out the champagne and some hors d'oeuvres. Before she could offer him a canapé, he settled himself on the love seat and tugged her down on his lap.

She'd meant the evening to be a quiet, enjoyable time. A prelude to her offer of marriage and to some lovemaking later on, but she'd underestimated the appeal of the night-gown.

She felt his body heat against her back, smelled his clean, masculine scent before he touched her shoulders. "We're lovers, you shouldn't be embarrassed."

"I'm not. I just wanted to talk to you, and I can't think when you're touching me."

"That's okay, baby. We'll talk later." He ran his hands over her torso, and Cass shivered. "Much later."

Cass leaned her head back against his shoulder and Rafe nibbled on her neck. She felt a return of that erratic pulse beat and was embarrassed at how easily he turned her on.

Rafe positioned her so that she was cradled across his lap. The back of her head rested on the arm of the love seat, and her body lay completely open to him. The hot, wet touch of his mouth moved down her neck and shoulders, following the low vee of the gown. She knew that he could see everything that nature had endowed her with. Could see her nipples hardening in anticipation of his touch. Could see the way her skin flushed with desire.

She arched her back when he reached the bottommost dip in the vee. His hands answered her unspoken plea, teasing and toying with her aroused flesh. She moaned low in her throat.

The touch of his fingers through the lace of the gown only caused more frustration. She shrugged her shoulders so that the strap of the gown fell down her arm. Rafe ignored her hint and continued to tease her through the material.

She grasped his head in her hands, pulling him up to her breast. Once there, Rafe took over. He suckled her nipple thoroughly. Cass felt the need to reciprocate his caresses and untucked his shirt from his jeans.

She burrowed her hands underneath the thin layer of cotton, needing to make him feel what she was feeling. More than that, she wanted to push him beyond the restraints he always showed when he made love to her. She needed to make him realize how much she loved him, would always love him.

She shoved the shirt up under his armpits and bent to kiss the flat male nipples hidden in the pelt of curly chest hair. Rafe straightened from her body, ripping the shirt over his head.

She bit and nipped at his flesh, teasing him the way he'd always teased her. Rafe's arm supported her back, holding her to his chest. He leaned against the back of the couch and groaned.

She slid from his lap and knelt between his knees.

Suddenly the languid mood that Rafe had been building in her snapped. She had to give him more of herself than she'd ever shared before. She had to show him how she really felt about him. She had to prove to him that she was his equal in all things, even this.

She laid her head on his lap, kissing the flesh along the edge of his jeans. She forayed beneath the waistband. He grabbed her head and pulled her body up onto his lap. Cass straddled his legs and knelt over him, so that he had to tilt his head back to kiss her.

The kiss was hot and heavy. Rafe thrust his tongue deep into her mouth before retreating and then repeating the process.

He grabbed her hips and forced her down onto his lap, directly over his groin. He arched off the couch while rubbing her against him. The sensation felt too good to be true. She fumbled for the fastenings of his jeans, needing to feel him against her, flesh to flesh.

Rafe held her wrist in a light grip and unfastened his jeans for her. He released her hands to pull her gown up over her hips. His fingers tested her, and she leaned forward to bite his neck gently.

"Oh, Rafe," she said on a sigh. She freed his long, hard

length from the jeans, and Rafe once again pulled her hands away from his body.

"Can you reach my back pocket?" He lifted his hips off the couch, and for the moment Cass reveled in the intimate contact.

"Cassie," he murmured, exasperated.

She reached around his hips, caressing the firm flesh of his buttocks as she searched his back pocket for the condom. She freed the foil packet and tore the package open. Rafe let her cover him with it and then pulled her head down to his. His tongue thrust past the barrier of her teeth at the same instant he entered her body.

The sensation sent fire coursing through her veins, and she bucked against him, aching to feel him all the way to her womb. Rafe controlled the pace, even though Cass was in the dominant position.

She decided that she wanted to be in control this once and tugged Rafe's hands from her hips. She joined their fingers together and held his hands loosely against the side of the couch. "Let me."

He released her hands and held on to her thighs, pushing them farther apart. She sank down on his length, then rose to repeat the motion. She rose and fell on him again and again. She felt her body quickening and Rafe's expanding. The climax was fast approaching, and she leaned forward to take his mouth. A second later they both hurtled over the edge. Cass collapsed against his shoulder breathing hoarsely and wondering why life had never felt this good before.

Rafe kissed her forehead and cuddled her close. "Damn, lady, you are magic."

"Oh, Rafe," she said, unable to form a coherent thought. She waited for her pulse to slow to a reasonable pace and rational thought to return. "Don't you wish we could be together always?"

He glanced up at her, his gray eyes free of all restraint.

She saw the caring in his eyes and somehow convinced herself that it must be love.

"Yeah, babe, I do."

"Marry me, Rafe," she said, softly dropping a kiss on his brow.

# Fourteen

At first Rafe was sure he'd misunderstood, but the soft look on Cass's face hadn't changed. The blood in his veins froze. He stopped breathing as he fought against the panic those few words evoked. *Marriage.* No way in hell, he thought, but couldn't say that out loud.

Cass looked so sweet and sure of what she wanted. Sure that he would say yes. Sure that he was the answer to her dreams, the missing link in her family. He tried to think of a nice way to turn her down. The problem wasn't that he didn't care for her, but that he cared too much.

But she wouldn't understand that. In fact, his reason made little rational sense even to him. He only knew that their relationship would be irrevocably changed if he married her.

"Why ruin a good thing?" he asked. As soon as the words were out of his mouth, he regretted them. He knew why Cass wanted marriage.

He wouldn't mind living with Cass. But marriage—that

was a step he didn't want to take. At the same time, his soul shriveled at the thought of spending his life alone. Maybe he could convince Cass to continue the way they had been.

He was honest enough to admit to himself that the main reason he didn't want marriage was that he was afraid of hurting her. He knew that eventually he'd turn into the same selfish bastard who'd unintentionally killed his own parents and sister.

As her lover, there was a limit to the things Cass would expect of him. She wouldn't expect him to help raise Andy. She wouldn't expect him to go to church with her. She wouldn't expect words of love that he knew he'd never be able to speak out loud.

Husbands were expected to do things that lovers weren't. Now he could help Cass with Andy when he wanted to, but he wasn't responsible for the boy all the time. And part-time lovers weren't expected to want children. The thought of his own children—children that were his and Cass's—scared the hell out of him. Almost as much as loving Cass did.

She stood up and straightened her nightgown, before crossing her arms over her breasts. He reached down and pulled off the condom and rezipped his pants. He strode out of the room to dispose of the condom. Damn, life had a way of smacking him with a two-by-four every time he started to feel complacent.

He walked back into the living room and discovered Cass wearing her trench coat. Was it because she no longer felt comfortable in only her nightgown with him. Rafe hurt in ways he hadn't thought he could at the sight of her wrapped in that long coat, covering herself from him. She wrapped it around her slim body like a shield. It wasn't just her body she covered but her heart as well.

She'd extinguished all of the candles, and the romantic music had stopped playing on the radio. He'd hurt her, and there wasn't a damned thing he could do to change it.

"Ah, hell, Cass. Why did you have to bring this up tonight? You know how I feel about marriage." He hated to hurt her, but there were certain corners in his life that had to be protected.

"I thought you'd changed your mind."

Rafe felt like a heel. The heartbreaking expression on her face was enough to make him long to change his mind. Tears made her ginger-colored eyes shine like polished pennies. Oh, damn, he was going to spend eternity in hell for this. He knew it.

Cass seemed to be crumbling right in front of him, and he knew he was to blame. He'd known all along that eventually he would hurt her, but there was no way he was going to bring another person into his family. He couldn't bury another Santini.

"I can't," he said softly. "If I made you my wife, Cass, and something happened to you..."

He stopped, not wanting to admit to something that he could hardly put into words. Cass walked to him then, hugging him tightly. Her soft curves sank perfectly into the rough contours of his body. Rafe knew that no other woman could ever fit him as perfectly.

He cursed himself for having given in to his desire for this woman. No matter how badly he'd wanted her, he'd had no right to ever touch her, kiss her or bury himself inside her. It wasn't fair to either one of them. A decent woman had a right to expect marriage, even in the crazy morality of the nineties.

Marriage was the last thing he wanted with Cass or any other woman. She didn't realize how destructive he could be without intending to.

The situation with Andy this afternoon could easily have gone the other way. There was only so long that he could second-guess what she wanted or needed from him. Only so long before he taught Andy something she wouldn't approve of. Only so long before he broke her heart and ruined her life.

"I won't let anything happen." Cass had the naive confidence of someone who believed in happy endings. Someone who thought that if you believed in a goal and tried hard enough to attain it, you would. But Rafe didn't believe that any longer. Hadn't for a long time.

"Cass, dammit, this isn't a game. I'm responsible for the deaths of my parents and my sister. I couldn't live with myself if the same thing happened to you and Andy." He caught her chin and tilted her face up to his. Tears clung to her lashes, and he felt the place in his soul that Cass had reawakened die a slow, painful death. Already he'd hurt her.

"You're not responsible for the death of your parents," she said, her voice husky with unshed tears.

"Yes, I am."

"Did you murder them?" she asked harshly.

"God, no."

She waited without saying a word. Her gaze intense, she'd held nothing back from him. Her proposal had left her vulnerable—emotionally naked in front of him, and he knew he owed her nothing less than the truth. But he was selfish enough not to want to see her look at him with disgust.

"My parents died in a car crash. My father's eyesight had been weakening for years, but the stubborn old man refused to wear glasses. We never let him drive at night, but Angelica had a recital and I was late to pick them up. In truth, I'd forgotten about picking them up, and the old man drove.

"They left late and he was hurrying. I don't know what happened. The roads were slick and wet—"

He couldn't go on. Suddenly, Cass's arms were around him, holding him, stroking him, telling him that everything would be okay.

But nothing would ever be okay.

"Ah, Cassie, you're so sweet. But you don't understand."

"The roads would still have been wet even if you'd driven."

"The wet road didn't kill them," he said.

"I don't understand."

"I know. I was late because I was with a woman. Someone I'd been intent on seducing and she'd finally succumbed. I ignored my responsibility to my family for my own selfish lust."

He thrust her away from him. He felt like the crude he was. Not good enough for this sweet, innocent woman standing in front of him. Not good enough to be a role model to her son. Not good enough to father a child with her. But, God, that was what he wanted—what he needed—to see her round with his child.

"But that wouldn't happen now."

"Yes, dammit it would. I have no control where you're concerned, and I swear if something happened to you...I can't take that chance."

Her eyes shuttered and she stepped away. She paced to the window and stood staring at the lace curtains. "I can't go on like this. I love you. But an affair goes against everything I've ever believed in."

At her words he almost hugged her tightly to his side. She loved him, he thought. His parents and sister had loved him too, but that hadn't prevented them from dying in a senseless car accident. An accident he could have prevented if he hadn't been selfish.

He wouldn't risk her life or Andy's on something that would probably burn out if they were forced to live together day to day. He hoped that the pain he caused her now would heal quickly. He forced himself to walk to her side. Touching her shoulder, he asked gently, "Then why did you let me in your bed?"

"I thought... I don't know. That things would work out in the end."

Her calm assumption that life would be fair annoyed him, because he knew that he'd ruin that belief for her before the night was over. "That's a damned infantile way of looking at life, Cass. There are no happy endings. Carl's death should have proven that to you."

She sighed and glanced away. "You're right."

"Dammit, lady, tell me we can go on the way we have been, or I'll leave here now."

"For good?"

"I can't go on hurting you like this. It's tearing me apart." She opened her mouth to reply, but Rafe silenced her with his fingers on her lips. "I wish I could change, Cassie, but I can't. I'm sorry."

She brushed his hand aside. "No, it's not your fault. I knew our relationship might not work out, but I had to try." Her voice cracked on the last word, and tears flowed steadily down her face. Rafe felt his own heart crack wide open.

He hauled her into his arms. "Ah, hell, Cass. I'd give anything to make it right for you."

She didn't say another word. She stood passively in his arms, crying silently. He released her when her tears were spent and dropped a kiss on the top of her head.

He had to leave. He had to sell the damn house he'd just bought. He had to get out of her life so that she could move on and find the man who could be all that she deserved.

"Goodbye, Cassie."

He walked out of the living room and into the dark night. He'd felt betrayed when his parents had died. Had felt broken when his sister had lingered for two weeks before dying, also. All his prayers, all his promises hadn't meant a damn thing. Life was a bitch.

Cass stared down at the picture she'd ordered enlarged and framed for Rafe. It was the three of them, taken on Thanksgiving Day. Her sister had captured Rafe smiling and looking like he was the king of the world. She'd originally planned to give it to him for Christmas, but now...it would only be a painful reminder of what could've been.

It hurt to see Rafe, to think of him, to keep on missing

him. Anger seethed in her, not the kind that caused rage, but a slow-burning resentment.

Cass knew that once the embarrassment faded, the anger would be uncontrollable. She didn't blame Rafe. He'd warned her in the beginning. It was her fault. She'd pinned her hopes on something she'd known he couldn't give. He'd told her often enough. But the knowledge didn't ease the heartache or the anger.

"Ma'am?"

Cass looked up at the sales clerk and realized that she'd been standing there, sighing. "How much do I owe you?"

She paid him and searched the store for Andy. He and Jeff had been getting along remarkably well, considering that three days ago they'd tried to beat each other up. On the first day Cass had taken the boys, they wouldn't even talk to each other, but boredom had forced them to become friends.

She found them and herded the boys to the grocery store next door. It was different having two children with her. Andy was usually so quiet and good that the new noise and friskiness was disturbing.

Tucking the brown package under her arm, Cass pulled a shopping cart out of the long line and backed into someone. The man steadied her. She turned to thank her rescuer and looked into Rafe's handsome face.

His minty breath brushed across her cheek, flooding her with memories of how he tasted. How he'd felt underneath her that last night. That night when she'd completely bared her soul to him and he'd rejected her.

She raised her gaze to his gray eyes. For a moment neither of them moved. Cass felt her body responding to his nearness and shifted to the side.

"Sorry," she muttered, and yanked on the cart handle, but the stubborn cart refused to budge. She'd hoped to escape quickly before Andy noticed their neighbor.

"Hi, Rafe." Andy had missed him the past few days.

The chance to talk to his hero while his new friend was there was apparently not one the boy would pass up.

"Hi, pal."

Andy glanced at Cass, a cautious question in his eyes. She nodded at him. She didn't want to be rude.

Cass listened to the exchange of voices but not the words of the conversation. Seeing Rafe hurt more than she'd thought it would. Being this close to him was like accidentally hitting a bruised knee on the coffee table. She knew the wound was there, but until she touched it, she could forget about the pain.

"Andy, come along, we have a lot of errands to run today," Cass refused to give in to the pleading look on her son's face. She felt like the evil stepmother in Cinderella, ruthlessly crushing her child.

She jerked the cart out of the line, and the package fell from under her arm. She felt like crying. Nothing was going right this week. She bent to retrieve the package and smacked her forehead into Rafe's. Pain shot down her brow, making her cry out. The man was hardheaded in more ways than one.

Rafe steadied her again, this time with a hand on her shoulder. "You okay?" he asked softly.

"I think so." It was one thing to be angry at him from afar, but when he was close like this, touching her, she wanted to be at peace with him. To lean into his touch and let him soothe away the pain in her head...and in her heart.

He helped her to her feet and then bent to pick up the package. "What's this?"

Cass felt her cheeks heat with a blush and reached for the package. "Nothing."

"Mom, I thought that was Rafe's Christmas present from us." Andy would try any tack to keep from leaving.

"Andrew," she said sharply. Her son glared at her, but backed away.

"I'm going to look at the comics." He didn't ask permission, which Cass knew was his retribution for her unwarranted anger. Jeff trailed behind Andy, and Cass watched them until they disappeared.

She held her hand out for the brown wrapped package, but Rafe didn't surrender it. "Rafe, please."

"What is this, Cass? What did you get me for Christmas?" His voice had taken on a husky note that brushed across her senses.

"Nothing that matters anymore. Can I have it back?" She held her hand out again.

"If it doesn't matter, why can't I see it?" The stubborn set of his jaw meant he wasn't backing down.

She shrugged. It wasn't like this was the first time she'd humiliated herself in front of this sophisticated man. Rafe opened the top of the parcel, then hesitated.

"Go ahead," she said. "You won't be happy until you find out what's in there."

He pulled out the frame wrapped in tissue paper and stared at it for a moment. He placed the wrapping paper in her cart and opened the protective layer of tissue. Cass stared down at her feet, not wanting to see his expression when he looked at her gift.

His sharply drawn breath brought Cass's head up. His eyes were filled with an unbearable pain. "Thank you, Cass. This means more than you'll ever know."

Cass couldn't handle it anymore. He'd cared for her, that much was obvious. But dammit, if he didn't intend to do anything about it, why couldn't he just leave her alone? She had to get away from him.

"I'm glad you like it," she snapped. Not the greatest thing anyone had ever said, but it was all she could think of. "Now, if you'll excuse me, I have some shopping to do."

"Cass, don't do this."

She paused in her frantic rush to leave him. She hated it, too. Did he think she wanted to stay away from him? "Don't do what, Rafe? You're the one who said it was over, remember?"

He cursed softly under his breath, but not so quietly that she didn't hear the word he'd used.

"For God's sake, stop that damned cursing all the time."

She turned the cart away from him and strode into the store. "Boys, follow me."

Andy and Jeff were quiet as Cass pushed the cart through the store. By the time they'd finished shopping, Rafe was long gone. Cass told herself she was thankful not to have to see him again. But she knew that part of her would always miss him.

She felt near tears, an aching mass of wounded emotions. God, she was never going to recover from losing him. This was worse than Carl's death, because that was final and irrevocable. Rafe was still living and breathing and right across the street, filling her with impossible hope.

It was the Friday before Christmas, and Rafe hadn't felt this lonely since his sister died. Cass had made him regret his decision, but Rafe refused to give in to her lures. If it was just him who would eventually be hurt he'd stay. But he knew that the longer their relationship continued the more pain he'd cause her.

Sure, she was everything any normal man would want, but he wasn't any woman's description of a "good catch." He swore too much, drank too much and he didn't know the first thing about child rearing. He sat on his porch, sipping coffee that didn't taste as good as Cass's.

Her old Volvo rattled down the street, and Rafe fingered the small, brown paper package in his hand. He tossed the remainder of his coffee into the bushes and motioned for Tundra to stay put.

He waited until Cass climbed out of the Volvo before leaving his yard. He crossed the street with slow, measured steps. He saw Cass tense when she saw him approaching. No matter how hard he tried to stay out of her life, he couldn't.

"Cass," he called as she stepped onto the porch.

She turned, her hazel eyes frozen and hard in the morning light. Her anger still hadn't died, and Rafe gave up any hope that Cass would change her mind and come back to him—the false hope he'd been harboring since he'd looked at that picture she'd ordered for him for Christmas.

It was a pipe dream anyway, but he hadn't expected to miss her so much. Staying away from her was the hardest thing he'd ever done in his life. He missed her, missed her laughter, her family, her love. The loss of his family had hurt deeply, but because of the permanency of their deaths, he hadn't continued to hope that they'd return. Even knowing it was useless, he couldn't help hoping Cass would change her mind.

"Yes?" she said stiffly. She braced her body as if expecting pain to be inflicted on her. He'd done that to her. Made her wary of the smallest gesture from him. He'd tried not to lead her on, but he had ignored problems that they should have faced before sleeping together. Before making love to her. Before letting her into his heart.

"I signed for this package." He handed her the small, brown wrapped box. The words sounded lame. He didn't tell her that he'd flagged the UPS man down and offered to sign for the package. He was a weak, pitiful excuse for a man, using any excuse to see her, to hear her voice again.

She hesitated, her small hand slowly closing around the box. He'd never noticed how small her hands were, but he remembered her soft touch on his body. He cursed under his breath, and Cass shot him a sharp glance.

"Raphael," she said in her best mother's voice. Her fingers brushed over the back of his hand, and desire shot through him, pooling in his groin. He jerked his hand back from the contact at the same time Cass did.

The package fell unheeded to the ground. Cass stared at him, and slowly the frozen look in her eyes disappeared. He groaned at the pained expression that replaced it. He'd never meant to harm her, hurt her...love her.

"Cassie," he said, reaching out to embrace her.

She stepped back, hitting her head on the Christmas wreath hanging on the front door. She wrapped her arms around her waist. "Please don't, Rafe."

He picked up the package and handed it to her, careful to stay out of touching range. He didn't want to cause her any more pain.

He turned to walk away and was stopped by her gentle touch on his back. "Thanks, Rafe."

"No problem, babe."

The phone started ringing and she shrugged her shoulders in an awkward movement.

"See ya around, Cass."

Rafe walked away without looking back, afraid that if he saw her wounded, ginger-colored eyes one more time, he'd break down and offer marriage, not because it was something he wanted, but because he couldn't bear to see her in pain.

A few minutes later Cass rushed out of the house. Rafe was on his way out for his morning jog with Tundra. He watched her jump into her car and speed down the street and wondered what had caused her to rush off.

Twenty minutes later Rafe was back from his jog. It hadn't helped that all he'd thought of was Cass. Her sweet, sexy body made him wonder why she'd been single since her husband's death. Her smile made him think of family and holidays. Her caring made him want to protect her from the harsh realities of life.

His phone rang as he headed down the hall to the shower. He grabbed the receiver and hopped from one foot to the other trying to step out of his shoes.

"Rafe, this is Iris, Cass's mom."

"Yes, Iris?" he asked, his heart in his throat.

"Cass has been in an accident. Could you pick Andy up from school?"

Rafe felt light-headed and sank down on to the bed. Cass injured, hurt, in physical danger. Iris was talking a mile a minute, and Rafe slowly understood her words. Punctured lung, broken ribs. Ah, hell.

"Where is she?"

"Orlando Regional Medical Center."

"I'll pick up Andy and meet you there."

Rafe hung up the phone and shoved his feet into the buffalo sandals he kept by the front door. Oh, God, please don't let her die.

# Fifteen

Rafe sat in the hospital waiting room staring blindly at a cheap print on the wall. He'd lied to Andy's school principal to get the boy released early. He'd told them he was Andy's stepfather, and damn if those words hadn't felt right in his mouth.

His lie was readily accepted for the truth, since he'd been in the office with Cass when she'd picked Andy up for fighting. It angered Rafe at how easily the school officials let the boy go with him. He filed that tidbit away to pursue later.

Rafe struggled with the knowledge that he really had no right to be there. That he'd given up that right two weeks ago when he'd rejected her marriage proposal. He'd move heaven and hell to have that right back.

The boy shifted beside him on the plastic chair. "Rafe?"

"Yes."

Andy had been quiet and withdrawn the entire drive over. His mother was still in surgery, and his grandmother was down the hall trying to get some sort of information on Cass's condition.

"Mom's not going to die, is she?"

"I don't know. That's what your grandma is trying to find out."

Rafe knew how it felt to have everyone in the world who loved you die. Knew what it was like to lose that security blanket, that one safeguard that you counted on always being there.

"I mean, you don't want her to leave, either, right? She's really missed you." Andy stared down at his lap. "I have, too."

Rafe froze, realizing at last that he'd let this boy become attached to him. He'd done it unintentionally, but as surely as if he'd planned to. He remembered the ball game, the fishing trip. Part of Rafe's soul had been longing for a child to spoil, to teach, to protect.

Rafe hadn't tried to insinuate himself in their lives or allow the Gambrels into his, but he had done it all the same. Cass and Andy were both needy, and they'd recognized that same need in him, refusing to let him stay out of their lives, to stay aloof and uninvolved as he'd always been.

Rafe realized now that he'd thrown away the chance of the lifetime. A chance to find what he had been missing for so long. A chance at happiness.

Andy reached out to him, then, his small hand brushing the back of his large callused one. Rafe wanted to promise Andy that he would protect Cass, that he'd keep her safe and that he'd make her well again. But he'd lived in the harsh realities of life too long to peddle a fairy tale on a little man. There were no guarantees.

Knowing that mere words would not comfort the boy, Rafe pulled him into a bear hug. He was not surprised by the feel of Andy's tears on his chest, but he hadn't expected them to affect him so deeply. He'd thought he was a loner, but that wasn't true anymore.

"You won't leave me will you, Rafe?" Andy asked, his voice shaky and unsure.

Rafe didn't hesitate; his days of running from involvement were over. "No, pal. I won't leave."

Andy pulled back and wiped his eyes with the back of his hand. "I love you, Rafe."

Rafe felt as if he'd been sucker punched. The affection was so unexpected, so…right. This is what had been missing from his life. A son and a wife, the family he'd always wanted to have until he'd lost his parents.

"I love you, too, Andy."

The kid hugged him again. "I hope they hurry up in there. I want to tell Mom. I think it'd be neat if you lived with us."

"I don't know. We'll have to check with Cass."

Iris came back a few minutes later. She held her pocketbook stiffly in one hand and a magazine in the other. Andy turned away to wipe the last traces of tears from his eyes.

"Any news?" Rafe asked, to draw her attention from the kid.

"She's stable and should be in the recovery room in thirty minutes. I told them to keep us posted."

"Thanks, Iris."

She sat down next to Andy, and the boy leaned over her shoulder to read the magazine.

"Come on, Andrew. Let's go and get some chocolate milk," she offered, and took her grandson by the hand, leading him down the hall.

Rafe stood and paced down the long corridor. It was empty and quiet. In the distance the low murmur of the nurse's voice at the station reached him. He remembered the long night he'd spent in the hospital after his parents' car accident. The guilt that he'd experienced had swamped him, making it nearly impossible to breathe. Rafe couldn't forget that he should have been the one driving that night. That his dad's eyesight was deteriorating. But the past couldn't be changed, and he admitted that the future could be. He was damned if he was going to let another day pass without living it to the fullest.

He'd stopped praying after his sister died. He'd forgotten about religion and the hope it offered. Forgotten that sometimes the only hope available was the belief in something that couldn't be seen or heard, only felt. Rafe found his way to the chapel.

Cass woke in a strange room. The total quiet of the room scared her. The low lighting left her disoriented. The scent was foreign to her. She hated not knowing where she was.

After a moment she realized she was in the hospital. Why? What had happened? The last thing she remembered was Rafe delivering that package. She'd wondered if he'd sent it. It wouldn't be the first time, but the package contained only clippings from the rose company.

She stretched on the uncomfortable bed. Cass groaned as pain pierced through her middle. She relaxed onto the pillows, deciding not to move again.

What the heck had happened? Her memory returned in a rush. She'd left the neighborhood in a hurry, unwilling to stay and watch Rafe next door. She remembered losing control of the car and spinning until the car crashed. She remembered the long ride to the hospital in the ambulance. Being so totally alone in the back of that emergency vehicle had brought home exactly how the rest of her life would be. Her life without Rafe.

Oh, heck, she missed him. And the knowledge that the only thing keeping them apart was her desire for marriage didn't help. She knew that Rafe wasn't the type of man to cheat on her. She knew that he wouldn't leave her without a good reason. And she knew that she couldn't live without him.

In her heart she knew there was only one solution. She had to decide what was more important. The way her church group looked at her, or the way that Rafe did. To

Rafe the ultimate in commitment was…she had no idea what his thoughts on commitment were.

Did he love her? She knew he cared. Had seen the pain in his eyes at the grocery store the day before and at her house this morning. She suspected he missed her. She wondered if the "missing" was a living, breathing pain that increased in sleep for him like it did with her.

She suspected that she wanted marriage because it was forever, binding. But she knew being married wasn't a guarantee for living happily ever after. Though she tended to only remember the good things about her marriage, she also knew there were fights, the constant togetherness and the yearning in Carl to be free.

She doubted it would be that way with Rafe. He was so much more than Carl had been. Not that she hadn't loved her first husband, but Rafe gave her everything he had. She knew there was honesty between the two of them. She knew that Rafe would never lie to her, because he hadn't when it had been in his favor to do so. She knew that she would never be as happy as she'd been with Rafe.

He'd shown her things she never took the time for, like simply sitting on the porch swing, or watching a live basketball game, playing with Tundra and fishing. He'd shown her a side of life that she hadn't expected to enjoy, but she had. He'd shown her his life, and she'd fallen in love with him.

Her near brush with death made her decide that having Rafe in her life was better than living without him. Life was too short, too complicated and too precious to waste.

As soon as she was able, she was going to find Rafe Santini and set things straight. He'd made her his woman and she'd be damned if she'd let him walk out of her life. She'd make him see that they belonged together. And if the only way she could have him was without marriage, then so be it.

"Cassandra?"

"Come in, Mom."

Her mother flicked on the overhead lights and came into the room on a cloud of Chanel. Cass reached for the controls to adjust the bed, but her mother took care of that for her.

Iris walked slowly around the bed, visually examining her daughter from head to foot. "Does anything hurt?"

"Everything, but I'll be fine. What happened?"

"You had a blowout and lost control of the car, according to the police officer. They'll be up later to take your statement."

"How's Andy?" It worried her, thinking of her son home alone, wondering where she was.

"Andy's scared, but holding up. That young man of yours is doing a fine job of helping Andy cope. Seeing you would be the best thing for the boy, but the doctor's refused to give me permission to bring him up."

"What man of mine?" Cass asked, unable to believe that Rafe would come to the hospital. He hated hospitals, and how would he have known to come? He wasn't on her emergency card, her mom was.

"Don't be a goose, Cassandra. I'm talking about Rafe Santini. I called him and asked him to pick up Andy before coming down here. Rafe and Andy are in the waiting room."

Cass was surprised, but decided that Rafe was too decent a man not to help out in an emergency. And he did care about her. She was glad he'd come.

"Do you need anything?" her mom asked.

"I'd like to see Andy and Rafe."

"I'll send Rafe up."

Her mom left as gracefully as she'd entered. Cass had always admired that trait in her mom, had often tried to imitate it, but never succeeded. She hand combed her hair, hoping that she didn't look like a storm refugee.

The door opened again and Andy walked in first, with Rafe behind him. Andy looked scared as he stared at her lying on the bed. She smiled at him and his little face lightened.

"Hi."

Her voice sounded dry and hoarse, and she immediately reached for the glass of water on the bedside table. Taking a small sip cleared her throat, and she felt better able to talk.

"Andy, how'd you get up here?"

"Rafe sneaked me in. Mom, are you okay?" Andy reached her side, trying to hug her, but the IV stand was in the way.

"I'm tired, but fine." She motioned for him to come around the other side, and hugged her son tightly.

"I thought you'd leave me, like Dad did."

"Not yet, honey."

Rafe stood next to the door, leaning against the wall. He seemed dark and dangerous, as he had on that day when she'd been trapped in the bathroom. But no amusement lurked in the background of those cold, gray eyes.

Cass ached for him, wondering if the hospital sights and sounds brought back a slew of bad memories. Cass hadn't expected him to come anywhere near the place much less up to her room. She remembered his parents' deaths were caused by a car accident.

Rafe arched one eyebrow at her when he met her gaze. She blushed, knowing she'd been caught staring at him once again. The man fascinated her.

"I better take Andy back downstairs before someone catches him up here." Rafe motioned for Andy.

Cass watched in amazement as Andy took Rafe's hand. Something good and wonderful had happened between them. A new bond had been formed and not one she'd ever be jealous of.

Rafe walked to the doorway.

"Rafe, will you come back?" God, she hoped so. There were so many things she wanted to tell him.

"Yeah," he said in a quiet tone before following Andy out the door.

Rafe took the stairs instead of the elevator back up to Cass's fourth-floor hospital room. He needed the time to regain his control. Her fragile form, lashed to the bed by IV and pulse-reading devices, made him remember his sister. She'd lingered for two weeks after the accident. Of course, she'd been in the intensive-care ward and not in a regular room like Cass.

Sweet, wonderful, beautiful Cass. He hesitated in front of her door, more nervous than he'd ever been before. He wiped his palms on the front of his jogging pants. He hadn't had a chance to change since he'd heard she'd been in the accident.

Before he was ready to go inside, the door opened and the nurse came out. "Hello, there. Go on in."

Rafe stepped inside. The door closed behind him with a soft whoosh. The sunlight streamed through the now-opened verticals. Cass was bathed in golden rays of sunlight.

She glanced in his direction, and Rafe froze. All his hopes cut to the quick. Cass looked at him like she looked at a stranger. No, a stranger would warrant curiosity, and he wasn't getting even that much from her. Dammit! He was too late. He'd left their relationship in the air too long. She'd resolved herself to a life alone.

"I wanted to talk to you." She motioned for him to come closer.

He strode toward the bed with purpose-filled strides. No way was he letting her brush him off without a fight. For once in his life he saw a chance at the future. A chance to really live instead of merely existing. A chance at happiness and love, and damned if he wasn't letting her go without a fight.

"Okay, Cass." He stood towering over her. Not wanting

to be comfortable, but ready to fight, to convince her to give him a chance at marriage.

She sat still for a few minutes, plucking at the bedsheet over her lap. Her hair was mussed from surgery and she wore no makeup, but she'd never looked more beautiful—more alive than she did at that moment.

"I've been doing a lot of thinking the last few hours. I've decided that—"

"Cass, there's something I want to tell you before you say anything else. I know that I've been a jerk and that I don't have the sense God gave an ox at times. But I do have a good job, and I'm learning to relate to kids."

"Rafe—"

"Don't interrupt." He paced to the window and stared out at the parking lot. He took a deep breath before crossing back to her side. "I'm trying to explain something here. I've never felt this way about a woman. At first I thought it was annoyance, then lust, now...ah, hell, Cassie."

"Don't cuss," she said softly.

He stared into her ginger-colored eyes and saw all the expression that had been missing before.

"What are you trying to say?"

"I had to lie to the principal at Andy's school."

"What did you tell him?"

"That I was Andy's stepfather. And it occurred to me that the lie sounded right—you know, true." Rafe thought about his words and how they might sound to Cass. He didn't want her to think he was marrying her because he wanted to have a son. He wanted to marry her because he couldn't live without her. Because every breath was somehow sweeter when she was standing next him. Because his soul flourished when she was around.

"Marry me."

There he'd said it. His hands were shaky, so he shoved them in his pockets. He tried to look casual, but his usual confidence had deserted him. He'd never proposed to a woman before.

"But, Rafe I thought you didn't want to get married. Why did you change your mind?"

No way was he going to be that vulnerable to this woman. "I just needed to think about it."

"Did my mother say something? Is it Andy? Do you suddenly want a child?"

He was hurting her again. Happiness had spread across her face, but now it died out like a falling star. Oh, God, he was losing her.

"I love you." He blurted the words out. "That's why I want to marry you."

Eyes wide with shock, she reached for him. Rafe stood over her for a minute, refusing to be drawn into her embrace. "I'm not a good catch. I'll understand if you've changed your mind."

"Rafe Santini, you're a perfectly good catch."

Cass sounded amused. He glared down at her for a second. "Babe, I'm serious."

"Rafe, I'm glad you came back." Cass had an expression of hope, desire and love on her face. In fact, he'd never seen a more joyous expression in the face of a woman. "You know I love you, and I'll agree to marry you if you're positive it's what you want. I'd hate for you to change your mind a few months down the road. I don't want you to leave again."

Rafe pulled her close to his side, loving the feel of her. He rubbed her back, dropping a petal-soft kiss on her brow. Grasping her chin, he lifted her face to his.

"Dammit, Cass. I won't change my mind. I don't want to waste the next fifty years of my life. And it will be wasted if you're not by my side."

She was silent for a minute. "You don't have to marry me. I don't mind living with you."

"Well, I mind." He hugged her closer to him, not wanting an inch of space between them. "Tell me you'll marry me."

"Okay," she said quickly. And just as he started to relax, she said, "Under one condition."

"What's that?"

"Tell me your middle name."

Rafe laughed. This woman brought more joy to his cold, lonely soul than he'd ever imagined. He leaned down and kissed her with all the love and passion in him. Kissed until they were hungry for breath. Kissed her until he forgot where he left off and she began.

"I'll tell you on our wedding night."

"No dice, Santini. It's now or never."

He kissed her again, hoping she'd drop the subject. He lifted his head to see her grinning and knew he was in trouble. "Genaro," he whispered in her ear.

"That's a fine name. I promise not to tell another living soul."

Rafe stared down at her twinkling eyes and knew that he'd never regret going to the rescue of a little boy and his distracting mother. He looked forward to being part of that family and expanding it.

"I think I should tell you that Andy already invited me to live with you."

"He did. What did you say?"

"That we'd have to check with you."

"Will you go get him? I want to share our good news."

"Ah, hell, babe. Anything for you."

"Someday, Rafe, I'm going to get you to stop cursing."

"It's harmless, honey."

She smiled at him as he walked out the door. Rafe carried that warmth in his heart. He knew now that the loneliness of the past three years was gone. Soon there'd be a slew of Santinis and Gambrels. A large, happy family all his own.

\* \* \* \* \*

# Take 4 bestselling love stories FREE

## Plus get a FREE surprise gift!

---

## Special Limited-time Offer

**Mail to Silhouette Reader Service™**

3010 Walden Avenue
P.O. Box 1867
Buffalo, N.Y. 14240-1867

**YES!** Please send me 4 free Silhouette Desire® novels and my free surprise gift. Then send me 6 brand-new novels every month, which I will receive months before they appear in bookstores. Bill me at the low price of $2.90 each plus 25¢ delivery and applicable sales tax, if any.* That's the complete price and a savings of over 10% off the cover prices—quite a bargain! I understand that accepting the books and gift places me under no obligation ever to buy any books. I can always return a shipment and cancel at any time. Even if I never buy another book from Silhouette, the 4 free books and the surprise gift are mine to keep forever.

225 BPA A3UU

| | |
|---|---|
| Name | (PLEASE PRINT) |
| Address | Apt. No. |
| City | State | Zip |

This offer is limited to one order per household and not valid to present Silhouette Desire® subscribers. *Terms and prices are subject to change without notice.
Sales tax applicable in N.Y.

UDES-696

©1990 Harlequin Enterprises Limited

# Help us celebrate 15 years of unforgettable romance with

## ▼ SILHOUETTE® ℨ Desire®

You could win a genuine lead crystal vase, or one of 4 sets of 4 crystal champagne flutes! Every prize is made of hand-blown, hand-cut crystal, with each process handled by master craftsmen. We're making these fantastic gifts available to be won by you, just for helping us celebrate 15 years of the best romance reading around!

## DESIRE CRYSTAL SWEEPSTAKES OFFICIAL ENTRY FORM

To enter, complete an Official Entry Form or 3" x 5" card by hand printing the words "Desire Crystal Sweepstakes," your name and address thereon and mailing it to: in the U.S., Desire Crystal Sweepstakes, P.O. Box 9076, Buffalo, NY 14269-9076; in Canada, Desire Crystal Sweepstakes, P.O. Box 637, Fort Erie, Ontario L2A 5X3. Limit: one entry per envelope, one prize to an individual, family or organization. Entries must be sent via first-class mail and be received no later than 12/31/97. No responsibility is assumed for lost, late, misdirected or nondelivered mail.

---

## DESIRE CRYSTAL SWEEPSTAKES
### OFFICIAL ENTRY FORM

Name: _____

Address: _____

City: _____

State/Prov.: _____  Zip/Postal Code: _____

KFO

---

15YRENTRY

# *Daniel MacGregor is at it again...*

### *New York Times* bestselling author

# NORA ROBERTS

introduces us to a new generation of MacGregors
as the lovable patriarch of the illustrious MacGregor
clan plays matchmaker again, this time to his three
gorgeous granddaughters in

# THE MACGREGOR BRIDES

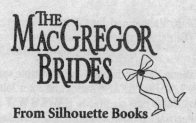

**From Silhouette Books**

Don't miss this brand-new continuation of Nora Roberts's
enormously popular *MacGregor* miniseries.

Available November 1997 at your favorite retail outlet.

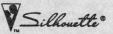

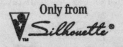

# SILHOUETTE DESIRE
## FIFTEEN YEARS OF FANTASY MEN!

Who can resist a Desire hero? No one! They're the men that fantasies are made of—handsome, rugged, caring and sexy. In November 1997 watch for:

**ANN MAJOR** as she continues her bestselling Children of Destiny series with *Nobody's Child.* This Man of the Month is a business tycoon who will melt your heart!

**Ranchin' Men!** In *Journey's End* by **BJ JAMES**, a rancher heals our soul-weary heroine with the power of love. This is part of BJ's bestselling series, The Black Watch. Talented author **EILEEN WILKS** is going to show us how *Cowboys Do It Best* in this sultry tale of seduction.

Marriage!
**LASS SMALL's** *How To Win (Back) a Wife* reunites an estranged married couple who fell out of love from a hasty wedding. A sexy attorney hears wedding bells in *Marriage on His Mind* by **SUSAN CROSBY**. And in *Wyoming Wife?* by **SHAWNA DELACORTE,** our hero has to convince a damsel in distress to be his bride.

**Silhouette Desire...what better way to meet so many gorgeous guys?**

Available November 1997, at your favorite retail outlet.

15YROCT

# SILHOUETTE WOMEN KNOW ROMANCE WHEN THEY SEE IT.

And they'll see it on **ROMANCE CLASSICS**, the new 24-hour TV channel devoted to romantic movies and original programs like the special **Romantically Speaking—Harlequin™ Goes Prime Time**.

**Romantically Speaking—Harlequin™ Goes Prime Time** introduces you to many of your favorite romance authors in a program developed exclusively for Harlequin® and Silhouette® readers.

Watch for **Romantically Speaking—Harlequin™ Goes Prime Time** beginning in the summer of 1997.

*If you're not receiving ROMANCE CLASSICS, call your local cable operator or satellite provider and ask for it today!*

### Escape to the network of your dreams.

See Ingrid Bergman and Gregory Peck in *Spellbound* on Romance Classics.

ROMANCE CLASSICS